THE TEARS
& SMILES
OF THINGS

stories, sketches, meditations

Ukrainian Studies

Series Editor: Vitaly Chernetsky (University of Kansas)

Other Titles in this Series:

"In the Tight Triangle of the Night":
The Early Poetry of Yuriy Tarnawsky (1956–1971),
between Modernism and Postmodernism
Maria Grazia Bartolini
Translated by Stanley Luczkiw

Cosmopolitan Spaces in Odesa: A Case Study
of an Urban Context
Edited by Mirja Lecke & Efraim Sicher

Dnipro: An Entangled History of a European City
Andrii Portnov

"Quiet Spiders of the Hidden Soul": Mykola (Nik)
Bazhan's Early Experimental Poetry
Edited by Oksana Rosenblum, Lev Fridman,
and Anzhelika Khyzhnya

THE TEARS & SMILES OF THINGS

stories, sketches, meditations

ANDRIY SODOMORA

translated from Ukrainian by Roman Ivashkiv & Sabrina Jaszi

BOSTON

2024

Library of Congress Control Number: 2023950284

English translation © Academic Studies Press, 2024

ISBN 9798887194370 hardback
ISBN 9798887194387 paperback
ISBN 9798887194394 Adobe PDF
ISBN 9798887194400 ePub

Published by Academic Studies Press
1577 Beacon St.
Brookline, MA 02446, USA
Tel: +1.617.782.6290

press@academicstudiespress.com
www.academicstudiespress.com

This book has been published with the
support of the Translate Ukraine Program

UKRAINIAN
//IIIBOOK
INSTITUTE

Contents

About the Author

The year 1962 saw—in addition to the appearance of Soviet missile bases in Cuba—the first translation in the former Soviet Union of Menander's *Dyskolos*, an ancient Greek comedy first performed in 316 BC. The play was translated into Ukrainian by the twenty-five-year-old Andriy Sodomora, who since then has served tirelessly as the Ukrainian "voice" of classical antiquity. Now Sodomora's original writing appears for the first time in English, immersing us once more in the universal wisdom of the ancients, while also sharing with us the most intimately described spaces and cadences of his homeland.

Sodomora's path to original writing has lasted, in his own words, an entire lifetime. He was born on December 1, 1937, in Vyriv, a village near western Ukrainian Lviv. His father Oleksandr was a Ukrainian Catholic priest, who participated in the Ukrainian national liberation movement in the 1920s, while his mother Sofiya helped establish a local branch of the Ukrainian Women's Union. In 1959, Andriy, the youngest of four children, graduated with a degree in classics from the Ivan Franko University of Lviv, where he is currently professor in the Department of Classical Philology.

Among those who inspired him to translate, Sodomora names his university professor Solomon Lurie, a Soviet Jewish classicist; Mykola Zerov, a neoclassicist poet and translator executed by the Soviets in 1937; and Borys Ten (pseudonym of Mykola Khomychevskyi), who translated *The Iliad* and *The Odyssey* into Ukrainian. Sodomora's phenomenal accomplishments over the last six decades bring him to the very top of the Ukrainian literary translation pantheon, along with Hryhoriy Kochur and Mykola Lukash, the two most prominent Ukrainian translators of all time, who also appear in his stories. His translation oeuvre includes an astounding number of volumes from ancient Greek and Roman authors (including Sophocles, Aeschylus, Euripides, Theogenis of Megara, Alcaeus of Mytilene, Hesiod, Archilochus, and Heraclitus, as well as Horace, Lucretius, Ovid, Virgil, Tibullus, Propertius, Cato the Elder, Sappho, Boethius, and Seneca, among others). Moreover, Sodomora has translated from Romance, Slavic, and Germanic languages, including works by Paul Verlaine and Federico García Lorca. Both as a scholar of antiquity and translator, he has demonstrated the continued vitality of ancient Greek and Roman cultures, claiming that "antiquity is alive" and that we just need to heed its message.

Since the late 1990s, Sodomora has written more than twenty books of original essays, poetry, and prose and won great critical acclaim for his literary studies and creative nonfiction. Guided by Seneca's advice to "hasten to find yourself first," today Sodomora successfully combines translation and creative writing and, at the age of eighty-five, remains extremely prolific. His love for and profound knowledge of the Ukrainian language and his "philological approach," with its particular attention to words, their histories and semantic layers, and to the soundscape of language, is manifested both in his scholarly and creative work.

Today, Sodomora still resides in Lviv where, since the beginning of Russia's full-scale invasion, he has written topical commentary and reflective essays for the zbruc.eu portal, applying his vast knowledge of classical literature and philosophy to current affairs. He believes that war is one of the greatest evils, but also recognizes that the horrors of war are compelling Ukrainians to reevaluate their patriotism as well as the importance of the Ukrainian language and Ukrainian culture. Sodomora, a member of the Shevchenko Scientific Society, is the winner of the Maksym Rylskyi translation prize (1986), the Antonovych Prize (2004), the Hryhoriy Kochur translation prize (2010), the UNESCO City of Literature Award (2019), and the BBC Ukraine Book of the Year Award (2021), among other accolades. In 2018, he was awarded the presidential "Order of Merit" for his contribution to Ukrainian culture.

What is significant about Sodomora's stories at this moment—when Russia is waging a genocidal war of aggression against Ukraine—is their depictions of Ukraine's distinctive history, both wide-ranging and finely detailed, and their inimitable sense of place. He shows western Ukrainian Lviv, a medieval city established in 1256, as a truly cosmopolitan place, while also giving us access to its most specific contours—from its cafés and apartments, to its archives and parks, to its geography and a single dying tree. Simultaneously, the stories, with their allusions to classical and world literature and their vast lexical repertoire that incorporates German and Polish, as well as Latin and Greek, demonstrate the diversity and worldliness of Ukrainian language and culture.

Introduction:
Old Wine in the
Evening Sunlight

Andriy Sodomora has long been renowned as Ukraine's pre-eminent translator of ancient Greek and Roman literatures, giving a Ukrainian voice to the classical canon: Hesiod, Menander, Greek lyric and tragic poets, Lucretius, Ovid, Virgil, Seneca, and Horace, among many others. Yet Sodomora has also gained recognition as a brilliant and original prose writer.

The current collection introduces this Sodomora to readers in English as an author of fiction in his own right. Even so, the voices of the authors who have been interpreted, translated, and internalized by Sodomora—their personalities, imagery, and ideas—inevitably reverberate in his own texts. In his stories, the world of classics mingles with the world of his own youth, adolescence, and adulthood, while his philologist's insight into language elucidates the world of things.

A classical philologist, Sodomora writes densely, in the style of his discipline; he doesn't just insert allusions to and quotations from the classics. His entire poetics is philological in nature as his lyrical protagonist's worldview is that of a philologist. Classical philology involves slow-motion reading, reread-ing, and plunging into the natural force of the text. Sodomora's prose enacts a similar slow-motion immersion into the world of things. While in his academic work Sodomora researches the poetics of individual words or phrases, in his fiction, he is primarily an archeologist of the word, who can snatch a line from an epic poem and weave around it an abundance of plots and dramas. Sodomora is most attracted to those words and lines that possess the richest literary history and have acquired the greatest number of contexts and senses, thereby incorporating the voices of various authors and the spirits of different epochs. He listens keenly to these polyphonic reverberations, unpacks them, and then presents them to the reader.* Interestingly, Sodomora's scholarly work often reflects the same elegiac, melancholy tone that is typical of his prose. His verbal reverberations are primarily about loss: of old meanings to which modern readers are often impervious, of images from previous epochs, of untranslatable nuances (for Sodomora sees translation as only an echo of the original text), and, broadly speaking, of the voices of bygone times and lost cultures.

***

It is no accident that this collection opens with a story entitled "Carpe Diem," in which Sodomora relies on Horace's famous "Ode to Leuconoe" (1.11) to portray an author who for him was one of the most important of antiquity. In the story, Horace is deep in thought, sitting on the shore, holding a glass of cold wine, and watching the sea on a winter evening. Unhurriedness reigns, accompanied by a soft soundscape and a delicate color palette. Like a tuning fork, "Carpe Diem" sets

---

*   Sodomora takes this approach in his book *Aforystychni etiudy* (Aphoristic etudes), whose central story "Carpe Diem" sets the tone for this collection.

the tone for the entire collection, which is meant to be read slowly so that each image can be intimately experienced. In pleasant company, Horace slowly sips his wine in the last rays of the setting sun as he listens to the monotone noise of the surf, not worried about tomorrow yet cognizant of the transience of today.

Sip by sip, scene by scene, story by story, the reader becomes *homo contemplans,** reflecting along with Sodomora on the fleeting nature of time and life. Sodomora shares with us, slowly and elegiacally, his internalized experiences with departing civilizations and generational change in one city and province at the crossroads of history in the eastern periphery of old Europe. His stories are set in the western Ukrainian city of Lviv or in the countryside of Halychyna (Galicia). But the many military, political, and cultural currents as well as the cataclysms that affected this part of the world in the twentieth century are echoed subtly in these "chamber" texts. Ultimately, echoes are at the foundation of Sodomora's tender and evanescent fictional world.

With each successive story, his seemingly hedonistic orientation towards the Dasein, the *being-there*, or *here-in-present*, acquires a more reflective valence and the perspective on the world becomes deeper and more complex. The author always lives in the moment but fills it with echoes from the past. His imagery is like wine whose flavors are richer with age, a wine that tastes best in the winter, at the end of day. To use a grammatical term, his present is not simply *praesens* but

---

*   A contemplating human, a concept from the philosophy of Horace and Epicurus.

praesens historicum, while history is not something that was and is no more, but rather something that we embrace and live.

***

In "At the Intersection," the author quotes two lines from his own poem "This salvaged moment is priceless, / for time is an echo of loss: It is us." For Sodomora, the past is like some phantom pain, a painful echo of something that will never return. It's a painful recollection of the self as it was and will never be again.

The structure of time in Sodomora becomes even more complicated because his narratives are premised not on these echoes but on his memories of them. What Sodomora depicts are echoes of echoes, memories of recollections, multilayered structures of temporal echoes, which allow him to create an especially fragile and tender world and to emphasize the feeling of loss and transience as something inevitable and primordial. For example, in the story "The Felled Shadow," a protagonist, no longer young, walks on a path he used to take daily in his youth and stops right by the place where, back in the day, a black locust used to cast a jagged shadow. In the protagonist's imagination, the shadow of the dry and dead tree is an echo of loss, which reminds the tree of its former vitality and green leaves. The black locust is gone. The shadow is gone. And even the old stump, which for some time served as a last reminder (echo) of an already inconspicuous detail in the city landscape, is gone. Decades later, "the felled shadow" sometimes reappears to the protagonist, now a more experienced man.

Sodomora, thus, writes not just about things per se, but about their "cut shadows." These are first and foremost shadows of our past selves. Time, here, is more than a cut shadow; it is "an echo of loss: It is us." Sodomora's recollections evoke his own youth,* then echo back to the current moment. We find ourselves in a Horatian (but really, Sodomorian) kind of living in the moment, which merges the distant and the near, objective and subjective, and ultimately, author and reader. Sodomora's imagery stems from intense emotions, loaded moments, and focal points at which all spatial and temporal dimensions intersect. Finally, all these echoes, shadows, reflections, and emotional experiences center on the authorial subject. We meet the man behind the stories as we read what he narrates.

***

Sometimes these concentrated experiences find a tangible and spatial embodiment in the mise-en-scène. For example, the story "The Flute" is set in a "cramped courtyard" where "a wedding dances itself out." The very verb *to dance out* reflects a leitmotif of this story and of the entire collection: fading and reverberating. We see a room on the top floor, the only one in the building where the light is still on (note the premonition of dimming), and above the courtyard "the deep-blue rectangle where a lonely star pulses."

Tension builds between these two poles (the courtyard, on the one hand, and the high window and star, on the other),

---

* "Hasten to find me, but hasten to find yourself first" is one of Sodomora's favorite maxims by Seneca.

giving rise to concentrated action. We hear the flute's voice, but we also see it soaring up the walls to reach the star. Upon reaching the window, however, it breaks and falls, only to attempt another ascent. The light from the star attracts the flute's music, but their "courtship" is suddenly interrupted by a brighter light from the top-floor window, which interrupts the music's flight, pulling it into the room. The light blends with a gust of wind, and the music becomes tangible, tactile: in a curtain's trembling and "the thinnest little thread of wavering smoke from a cigarette."

This dialogue playing out in the courtyard blends different sensory experiences (i.e., music, light, and wind) and also extends the boundaries of time and space. The wind brings with it "a breath" of the classical Golden Age, while music, wind, and light together conjure up images from the primeval days when their union first manifested: when the evening's first star appeared in the sky, the flute's forefather the reed rustled in response to the touch of Wind, eternal ruler of space. The tender and evanescent image of music created by the wind and the star encapsulates the entire cosmos in all of its temporal and spatial infinity.

But there is another storyline in "The Flute," hidden in a picture where "the dark silhouette of a woman walks down a snowy path into the depths of a park [. . .] a receding figure—getting smaller, but still not vanishing from the snow-filled expanse." This storyline is just as tender and elusive (a silhouette vanishing into the snow) and just as fleeting (a retreat into the distance). It reverberates with the flute's fading voice, and the two blend into a single weakening impulse that slowly dims and goes silent. It is absorbed into the tight space of the courtyard well, merging in a single gust with the flute's flickering song.

The flute's music is a superb example of Sodomora's condensation of a fleeting moment into a single image. Sodomora captures it for us in the mouth of the well, establishing a point of focus for the lyrical protagonist and for the reader. In his stories we see many examples of this concentric arrangement of space, and of the condensation of the past and its echoes into spaces. He merges visual, aural, and olfactory images in his descriptions, and this sensuality is a trademark of Somodora's style. Phantoms surface from the darkness, then plunge back into it so that traces of all centuries are combined.

***

Sodomora's stories typically unveil a slow-motion reality that allows him to fill the moment with all kinds of detail as well as with different perspectives, dimensions, and temporalities. The drama in "Dead Silence," for example, reaches its culmination on a sleepless moon-lit night at the moment the protagonist finally manages to doze off, while the moon travels a short distance from the window's crossbeams to its edge. Painting a cross on the wall, the moonlight unites with the dying groans of an old woman next door in an eerie symphony. It then pales as the dying woman's last sighs are swallowed by the night's silence. Here again, the reader is subsumed in a medley of fading, silencing, and echoing. The moon, itself a protagonist and "tuning fork" in this drama, can be seen twice: reflected on the wall of the building across the street and passing through the window's top quadrant. This moon, which lights both the protagonist's and the dying woman's rooms, synaesthetically fills the former with the voice of death and then with a dead cosmic silence. Sodomora condenses all of these spaces behind windows and walls, fitting all the light and cosmos into a single dot, and shows it to us like a shadow play.

Such indirect depiction is one of Sodomora's recurrent literary devices. The temporal and spatial remoteness and partitioning of his images contribute to his signature philosophical distance and melancholy-meditative detachment. In this way, he softens and harmonizes tragedy and pain, which only echo in his sketches and never scream out. Sodomora is a master of dealing with tragedy in a discrete and subdued manner.

***

Concentric space plays an important role in Sodomora's fictional world. It performs several simultaneous functions and works differently across his stories. We've already seen how it amplifies and concentrates temporally and spatially disparate images, or rather their echoes. But the boundaries of this space also work as a kind of filter, for example, in "Dead Silence," where the protagonist is fenced off by the four walls of his room from all the cosmic and private tragedies, and the room is filled only with their echoes. A similar "filtering" function is attributed to fog and rain in other stories, "when, in a blur of space and time, the usual 'here and now' loses its reality" and when "from the rain's monotone whisper, intercepted by the umbrella" some voices of the past come through, and the more quiet they are, the more distinct.

In the quote above, from "The Language of Rain," we find another illustration of concentric space: the space under the umbrella "delicately defined by falling droplets." Described as "the most modest of nomadic dwellings," it "squires its recluse-tenant through the rainy city's streets and squares" while "its illusory coziness encourages contemplation . . ." This concentric space includes a resonator (the umbrella's covering not only captures and intensifies the noise of the rain but calls in echoes of the past); a softening filter; and, finally, a third function, that of separating its owner from external stimuli, which allow him to plunge into his interior world, to fill the moment with internal depth as well as with vertical personal contexts—to concentrate.

We can see here why Sodomora is so smitten with shadows, drizzle, grayness, and rain. They create a shroud that protects the narrator from the external world and all of its hastiness, brightness, hubbub, and kaleidoscopic range. The shield of fog allows him to sink into himself, as though hypnotized and half-dreaming, to truly feel the condensed moment. Such drizzle, rain, darkness, and fog seem to dissolve spatial and temporal boundaries, allowing different dimensions to converge in a single place, forming one voluminous reverberation of loss. In cordoning spaces off with rain and fog, Sodomora slows us down to go deep into subtle internal shifts that are saturated with reflections and reverberations.

***

In his stories, Sodomora is ever the philologist, transitioning from the poetics of words to the poetics of objects. His meditative sketches move slowly, to the point almost of stillness, while he attends to living through a particular moment and uncovering all of its archeological layers, in the deliberate concentration of a close philological reading that fixates on individual phrases and words. While his academic research often focuses on a particular word or phrase, his creative work continues to build fictional worlds around the objects and impressions snatched from his surroundings. Sodomora explores them carefully, replenishes their lost meanings, uncovers their forgotten layers, and refreshes our memory with their old and lost contexts.

In many stories in this collection, the emphasis is on individual objects: old, abandoned, lost, inconspicuous things that still remember the warmth of their last owner's hands or remind us of a household task that has fallen into oblivion in the new epoch. Sodomora poeticizes these inconsequential, random, and abandoned things that are lost in the inter-time, between epochs and dimensions (cf. "The World between the Windowpanes" or "The Owl"). He can convey their fading warmth, the spirit of a previous epoch, so impalpable to younger generations. For him, these objects are like Ray Bradbury's dandelion wine. He uncorks the summer trapped within, and shares it with his readers in wintertime. Sodomora knows how to delay the imminent departure of things and sensations, as if he is their last guardian, seeing the echoes of the past off into oblivion.

***

Yet Sodomora's sketches are so much more than "a museum of abandoned things."* He also creates a gallery of "abandoned people," all of them are shadows of some bygone epoch, part

---

*   An allusion to Oksana Zabuzhko's novel *The Museum of Abandoned Secrets*.

of the strata of old Lviv's diverse multiethnic population that by some strange accident still resides in post-World War II Lviv, now a completely different city. Their modest apartments serve as time capsules for the spirits of old times. We sense that this world is doomed, and that Sodomora is its sole custodian. He is the only one still able to recall the shadow of a black locust tree, cut a dozen years ago; the only one who takes note of a holy fool's whirligig at the windy autumn crossroads in a neighborhood on the city's outskirts, which has long since been rebuilt.

The insignificant people and things depicted by Sodomora are not only the last inhabitants of the old world, but, most importantly, of the internal world of "homo sentiens." Every generation bears the spirit of its epoch, which recedes as it passes on. We too are bearers of an internal world and its reverberations, a world that will disappear when we depart. Sodomora focuses on the transience of these worlds, individual worlds against the passing of entire epochs, and while doing so he manages to pack a complex idea of transience into Horace's and Epicurus's seemingly lighthearted and hedonistic phrase *carpe diem*—living in the moment, living through the experience of the moment.

***

The stories selected here from *The Tears of Things* are dominated by gray colors, dim imagery, and notions of fading and disappearing. They are imbued with echoes of the past: old age and abandoned things, people and objects that find themselves in unfamiliar contexts where they are trapped alone with time. A different landscape is unveiled in the stories chosen from the later collection entitled *The Smiles of Things*, which present a world seen by a child, full of bright colors and first impressions. Here, Sodomora creates a lively and vivid amalgamation of fresh sensations and images, giving these sketches the feel of a cosmogony—the birth of a new world. People and things still end up where they belong, in their natural contexts, but instead of sorrow over loss, we sense the joy of achievement. Through a child's eyes we often see—this time in bright tones—the same old world portrayed in *The Tears*. In a sense, *The Smiles* is a prequel to *The Tears*: it introduces us to the time when the dandelions have barely bloomed, before Sodomora uncorks his "dandelion wine" for us. *The Smiles* is nonetheless inflected by a radiant melancholy. Although the focus is a time before the loss, these are still the recollections of an older person. Their radiance masks a tragic note not present in *The Tears*: immersion in the world of childhood is perhaps not simply as a return to beginnings, but the logical completion of the life cycle, a melancholic return home, "before moving further"...

Markiyan Dombrovskyi

Translators' Introductions

It's August 2023 as I write my introduction, and August is a month of celebrating women in translation. I want to start by highlighting this, as although the author translated here is a man, it is primarily thanks to the women I have been fortunate to meet and work with in my life—translators, writers, editors, scholars, and mentors—that this translation has been possible.

My own desire to translate Andriy Sodomora was sparked by the late Roksolana Petrivna Zorivchak, Professor and Chair in the Hryhoriy Kochur Department of Translation Studies at the Ivan Franko National University of Lviv, Ukraine. In the early 2000s, when I was her student, Roksolana Petrivna (that's how we addressed her) would repeatedly bring up Sodomora's name in class, speaking with great admiration of his translations and scholarship. Above all, she emphasized Sodomora's Ukrainian, which to us was a less impressive fact because, as native speakers, we were convinced we knew Ukrainian well enough. Sodomora was a brilliant public speaker and the most erudite intellectual we had the privilege of knowing in person at that time. For us, he was a deity of sorts, a translation god from antiquity, whose relevance he never tired of underscoring.

Many years later, when I started exploring the world of literary translation, Roksolana Petrivna suggested I try my hand at translating one or two of Sodomora's own stories. Although translations from Ukrainian into English were then increasingly being published, not a single English translation of Sodomora's work was available. I gladly agreed, without quite realizing what I was getting myself into. Translation is by default a daunting task that involves, among other things, dealing with linguistic asymmetries, understanding cultural differences, accounting for political contexts, appreciating aesthetic nuances, and reconciling divergent sensibilities. Translating Sodomora was all this and more: It turned out to be a task that reminds me of Jacques Derrida's words on translation—simultaneously necessary and impossible.

The first story on which I worked was "Syvyi viter," or "The Silver-Haired Wind," and it proved to be as challenging as I had suspected. The story starts with a seemingly simple description of the wind; the opening adjective *nalitnyi* not only lacked an English equivalent but wasn't in Ukrainian dictionaries either. Although contextually understandable, it is not a common modifier in Ukrainian. After some research, I managed to locate the word in Mykola Zerov's Ukrainian translation of Horace's Ode 3.30 ("Exegi monumentum aere perennius").* Describing the monument he erected, Horace claims that it will never be destroyed by rain or wind, the Latin word for the latter being *Aquilo*, a stormy northern wind. In the available English translations, the epithets modifying *the wind* range from "vain" and "ungovernable" to "obstreperous," "fierce," and "raging," to mention but a few. In Zerov, this wind is *nalitnyi*, a word that can be roughly translated into English—if inelegantly and verbosely—as

---

* Horace is one of Sodomora's favorite writers, while Zerov, an early twentieth-century neoclassicist poet, scholar, and translator, was a great influence.

"one that blows suddenly and attacks." This presented me with a dilemma. Some might argue that it's only a word, and there's much more to the story, which is correct, but for me this small conundrum served as a reminder that a pursuit of "sameness" in translation is ultimately futile, that translation is after all about difference, and that the focus should be on trying to create, rather than "recreate," a work of art in its own right. And so my translator's journey through Sodomora's texts and intertexts, a journey through the thickets of untranslatability, began . . .

As a teacher of literary translation, I always emphasize that translation is about gain rather than loss. As I translated Sodomora, I had to admit to myself that this is much easier theorized than done. Throughout the process, I often felt that crucial nuances of the Ukrainian original ended up impoverished (and I don't like this word at all) in English. In his opening essay, "People amidst Things," Sodomora unravels the beautiful ambiguity of Virgil's phrase "sunt lacrimae rerum" (there are tears *of* things), from which the title is derived. In practical terms, one had to choose a suitable English preposition for the "prepositionless" Latin genitive case—a choice that goes back to the interpretive problem (i.e., tears *of* things? or tears *for* things? *in* things? or some other option?). But it was, in the end, "the smiles of things" that posed a greater difficulty. Sodomora does not quite say *smiles* in Ukrainian. Instead, he uses a rather rare lexeme *usmikh*, a synonymous singular word of higher register with a more mature feel (something along the lines of *nostalgic smile*) that, not surprisingly, has no corresponding word in English. Thus, in translating word after word, I had the nagging feeling that my simplistic English pales compared to Sodomora's rich sophisticated Ukrainian. To be fair, I recognized the fact that, like his great predecessors (Kochur, Lukash, and Zerov, among others), Sodomora takes every opportunity, both in his translations and original work, to "teach" his readers more refined Ukrainian, a language he loves dearly and one that has been ruthlessly oppressed and eradicated by Ruzzia for centuries. That this peculiar didactic function could simply not be captured in English (and it's not what anglophone readers would expect from a translation) was of little consolation.

Grammatical differences between English and Ukrainian continued to creep up on me at the most inopportune moments as if to remind me of the inseparability of form and content, which I naively hoped would be less problematic in prose than it is in poetry. In the story *"Praesens Historicum,"* for example, Sodomora cites a maxim about the relevance of history in our lives, about the importance of remembering and cherishing the past. He writes, "khto ne zhyve mynulym, toi vzahali ne zhyve," which can be translated verbatim as "who doesn't live the past, doesn't live at all." Grammatically, the construction relies on the instrumental case of the Ukrainian word for *past, mynulym.* Its function—marking an indirect object used as an instrument or tool, similar to "by means of"—is normally conveyed in English, depending on context, by the prepositions *with* or *by* (as in *write with a pen* or *drive by car*, for instance). Each of these prepositions, however, would add unintended meanings. Opting for other verbs instead, even if they fit contextually (as in *to embrace* the past) affects the sentence's parallel structure, based on repetition of the verb *to live.*

From there, the challenges became increasingly complex, involving puns, transmesis (fictional portrayals of the process of translation or translator-characters), and even poetry— both his own and that of others—which Sodomora often incorporates into his stories. The story "The Felled Shadow" is inspired by Federico García Lorca's "Canción del naranjo seco" ("The Song of the Barren Orange Tree") with a brilliant (very touching and euphemistic) opening line: "Leñador. / Córtame la sombra" ("Woodcutter, / cut down my shadow!"). Sodomora's protagonist remembers a dying black locust and debates, in his imagination, with García Lorca's Ukrainian translator Mykola Lukash on translation choices. He then continues to explore a mesmerizing amalgam of the visual and the auditory by focusing on the ambivalence of the Ukrainian word *tin'*, which stands for *shadow* but at the same time is an onomatopoeic word for the sound produced by the axe cutting a tree. Capturing wordplay of this caliber, when form is so intricately interwoven with semantics across multiple intertexts, is indeed a nearly impossible task.

As in "The Felled Shadow," sound and transmesis are two of the crucial elements of "In the Language of Rain," whose protagonist, spellbound by the rain's whisper, creates a poem, alluding to Verlaine and Rimbaud and ruminating over poetry and translation. To complicate things further, the story then introduces us to the protagonist's friend, who addresses him in Polish (a language understood and spoken by many in western Ukraine), although both could actually speak Ukrainian, and this, in turn, invites another reflection in the story on the problem of sameness in translation. To Sodomora, the greeting worked only in Polish, but not in Ukrainian, despite them being cognate Slavic languages. This story, therefore, reminds us of Derrida's admonition in his "Shibboleth for Paul Celan." He writes, "Everything seems in principle, by right, translatable except for the mark of the difference among the languages within the same poetic event" (qtd. in Kathleen Davis's 1997 essay "Signature in translation" in Dirk Delabastita's edited volume *Traductio: Essays on Punning and Translation*).

Such challenges accumulated and made it painfully obvious to me that if creating a work of art (rather than merely a pale copy of Sodomora's original) was indeed the goal, I needed help. A firm believer in collaborative translation, I was lucky that Sabrina Jaszi (who was once my student but at that time already an accomplished writer and translator, pursuing doctoral studies at UC Berkeley) kindly agreed, also without knowing what she was getting herself into, to work together. Since translation is a two-fold act that consists first of the most intimate reading and then of creative writing, Sabrina and I felt that we complemented each other well, without dividing the job strictly along these lines. Countless hours were spent on zoom (re)reading and (re)writing, and I will be forever grateful to Sabrina, my collaborator and friend, for not only being extremely patient with me (despite my constantly irritating efforts to hog the covers in the direction I thought was "Sodomora's way") but, first and foremost, for making sure that Sodomora's stories are as scintillating in English as they are in Ukrainian. Unlike myself, who is primarily a scholar of Ukrainian/Slavic and translation studies, Sabrina is, above all, a writer whose flair for English and ingenuity helped to ensure that our translation not only captures what Sodomora says but gives readers a taste of how he says it.

Finally, the last person without whom I cannot imagine completing the task is Erín Moure, a brilliant Canadian writer and translator, whom I have been extremely fortunate to have as my mentor and whose advice and encouragement have always improved my work. Her feedback on the stories has been invaluable, especially when it came to poetry and when Sabrina and I were wrestling with other instances of the nearly untranslatable.

The journey of translating Sodomora was arduous, but now that the job is almost finished it feels extremely rewarding. Recalling Roksolana Petrivna's initial suggestion all those years ago to translate a story or two, I now realize that in addition to trying to make Sodomora's Ukrainian gems available to a wider audience, she also wanted to give me a gift of discovering a path to myself . . . For what is translation if not an attempt to understand the Other, to share with others, and to find a path back to one's own self?

Roman Ivashkiv

***

Every translation is collaborative, since it involves a real or imagined dialogue with the author. However, translating the prose pieces contained within this collection initiated a number of concurrent conversations: with the original work and its ancient and modern intertexts, with Sodomora, and with my co-translator Roman Ivashkiv. As a native speaker of English, but knowing only basic Ukrainian, my role in this collective was to produce draft translations that Roman and I would then correct, rewrite, and argue over. Roman was my guide through the intricacies of Ukrainian language and culture and my fellow student when approaching the literary and philosophical abundance of Sodomora's writing. I translated for the reader, trying to make Sodmora's sentences beautiful and legible in a new language, and also for Sodomora whose own rather audacious approach to translation I came to appreciate through his texts. Roman often pushed back, ruffling my smooth translations and reinserting words or syntax that were uniquely Ukrainian or uniquely Sodomorian. Phrases so solidly implanted in my native speaker's English sometimes lost their purchase. What resulted was a more porous English through which Sodomora's synesthetic and transtemporal imaginings could seep.

So vivid are Sodmora's sensations and locations that they have attached themselves to my own memories working closely on their translation: I have listened at night as a "flickering scale reverberates in the stone symphony" of my town. I have eaten summer strawberries, myself recalling "dizzying antiquity, when there was no man to inhale [the strawberries], when the ferns were colossal, when dinosaurs trampled the grasses . . ." Smells are particularly potent in Sodomora's writing. The translation of one such scent illustrates the vitality of Sodomora's sensual impressions as well as my process translating them.

From a musty attic stacked with Hapsburg curios to Bera pears "yellowing, softening, and filling up with malt" in the little "orchard-paradise" of Sodomora's Vyriv childhood, smells transport Sodomora far beyond the finite geography of his stories' settings. And at one time when I was translating these pieces, I too was preoccupied by scents: In the first trimester of pregnancy, my olfactory senses intensified and I began to experience the world more as Sodomora must, with smells so powerful that they demand strong words and poetry. Sulfurous broccoli sent me running to the street and sickly, camphorous eucalyptus made me gasp. Most of all, my world reeked of coffee, brewed in my doorless kitchen, or the cafes where I went to escape my apartment with all of its sickening old-new aromas. Coffee also wafted from Sodomora's pages: Since the early nineteenth century his home city of Liviv has had the reputation of a coffee capital and coffee appears in several of his stories from the region.

In "My Mother's Smile," the morning routine of coffee-making calls up spectral memories of the narrator's mother. I was faced with a dilemma, however, since Sodomora's take on the smell of coffee, an aroma both subtle (*tonkyi*) and penetrating, conflicted with my own. Given my strong distaste for coffee, I could not think of translating Sodomora's *tonkyi* as "subtle" or, even worse, "delicate." I tried to come up with workarounds: The literal meaning of *tonkyi* is "thin, narrow," so perhaps he intends something like "sharp," I thought, trying to square Sodomora's impressions with my own. Why was Sodomora, always so perceptive, suddenly inaccurate?

The narrator of "My Mother's Smile" struggles to recall a face and an expression from his childhood. The smile is the story's namesake and subject matter—and yet, whenever the narrator tries to imagine it, his mother turns away. This duality—Sodomora's obsession with the memory and its evanescence—finally helped me render coffee's aroma in the story. Thinned by time like the fleeting smile, it is as inaccessible in his thoughts as it is omnipresent. Roman and I settled on the following translation, which created the space for opposite impressions: "As soon as it is pushed out of the grinder, the fine aroma of ground coffee permeates the entire house." In this wording, "fine" could mean "thin, delicate" or, alternately, "exquisite, first-class."

It can be tempting to view translation as a set of problems: finding the right word; eliminating contradiction; banishing shadows and elucidating. But in approaching Sodomora's world of glimmering opacity, the task, more often, was to cultivate its murky half-light. This was aided by our process of collaboration, within which no demystified reading or rewriting of the work was ever possible.

Sabrina Jaszi

A Note on Translation

In crafting our translation, we have endeavored both to bring Sodomora's writing to readers and to bring readers to his sophisticated writing, which is idiosyncratic and challenging even to readers of Ukrainian. Sodomora's inventive syntax is marked by elaborate sentence structure, emphatic inversion, and long compound sentences. We have attempted to preserve some of these structures without compromising the playfulness and lucidity of thought underlying them. The same is true for our approach to punctuation: Sodomora is fond of em-dashes, which serve multiple purposes, and of ellipses, which invite readers to pause and reflect. Occasionally, Sodomora employs footnotes, which have been preserved in our translation. His frequent allusions and references to other authors and philosophers are explained in endnotes, which we also use to cite sources, provide metacommentary on translation (as both a practice and a literary subject) and give cultural context. A brief glossary explains certain terms that may be unfamiliar to the reader. In transliterating Ukrainian words, we have followed the modified Library of Congress system. For English translations of ancient Greek and Roman works frequently quoted by Sodomora, we referred most often to the Loeb Classical Library, while the Internet Encyclopedia of Ukraine served as a starting point for information related to Ukrainian culture.

The Tears and Smiles of Things

Stories, Sketches, Meditations

In Lieu of a Preface:
People amidst Things

> In my heart I remember only my childhood; nothing else belongs to me.
>
> (Ivan Bunin)[1]

A person lives amidst people (*homo inter homines*), but also amidst things. And people are journeying, not only to other people, but also to things. Thus, to their own selves. For things are not just physical objects that we can touch — they are everything in the world: our actions, thoughts, and feelings. They are "things" and they are reality. The Latin *res* means *thing*, while *realis* means *material* (i.e., *thing-like*), or real. Lucretius's poem *On the Nature of Things* is, fundamentally, about the natural world. Virgil goes further. Having sailed to Carthage and seen in one of the temples images of the Trojan War, his Aeneas uttered the famous words: "There are tears of things, and earthly things touch the heart."[2] Here, *things* are, strictly speaking, the events that people mourn. Hardly any other phrase has gotten such a wide response in the European philosophical discourse as Virgil's: "Sunt lacrimae rerum . . ."—"There are tears of things," or, more precisely, "Tears are in the nature of things." According to Victor Hugo, in this phrase—a drop of infinity in its complex condensed sublimity—Virgil encapsulated all the fatalism of antiquity and foresaw all the melancholy of the modern era.

In this phrase, we find one of the most forward-looking poetic formulations, that—thanks to its "mysterious ambiguity"—is receptive to new meanings, shades, and moods. This ambiguity comes, in turn, from the polysemy of the Latin word *res*, primarily associated with the interpretation of *thing* as object. In fact, Virgil implies that things have a psychic aura, a soul (and where there's a soul, there are tears). For instance, as Ray Bradbury's astronaut from the distant future says: "Ask me, then, if I believe in the spirit of the things as they were used, and I'll say yes . . ."[3]

There are people's tears for things that disappear, but also the tears of objects for people who are shorter-lived than things themselves. Virgil's shepherd, as he was passing on from life, gave his reed pipe away with the words: "Now it claims you as its second master."[4] The reed pipe has someone new, but may still long for its former owner, who imparted their soul to it. In an old Ukrainian folk song, a pipe player is survived by their instrument that then changes hands. And for some people, things are only that which can be touched by the hand—not by the soul. So tears are in the nature of things. But so are smiles. And they belong to our childhood, to the things that surrounded us, that shaped our souls, the things to which we were intimately attached.

The Ukrainian verb "to worry" is composed of the prefix "re" and the root "to live." So the Ukrainian phrase "don't worry" dissuades us from "re-living"—that is, rehashing some moment from the past or dwelling on it. We can "re-live" our lives, though, the way we reread a book. The sweetest pages of this book are childhood. For back then, everything was new—miraculous and smiling. With time, it all becomes commonplace; a miracle no longer appears as such, though it remains miraculous. You just have to look closely . . . It's important to keep journeying toward those things, and consequently toward our own selves. For what is the soul, if not a mass of threads that tie us not only to the world of nature but to the world of objects? These "threads" are the strings of the soul, its tunes and intonations.

Because of the times we live in, those threads are cut, or, rather, we cut them, we remove the strings: It's no longer God's world we're speaking with, but the man-made, virtual one. Even those things that served us and made it into our souls, things that themselves had souls, depart: pencils, pens, ink, and notebooks. The book gives way to the tablet, the metal key to the electronic one, not to mention an array of tools: the millstone, the mortar, the hemp-brake, the sickle, the washboard, the flatiron.

Everything slowly blurs, no longer real, but a simulacrum: The slang expression "like" didn't just appear out of the blue. Neither did "anyway." For although you can't just take *any* way from the corn kernel deposited in the furrow to aromatic *kulesha* (corn porridge), or to *palianytsia* (flatbread), somehow there is popcorn. People seem to have disconnected themselves from the living world of nature, and the five "scouts" (as John Amos Comenius called the senses[5]) are left idle, providing no sustenance to the soul: Where can they go in an urbanized, technological world of stone, plastic, and glass? What can they report back to humans, who, like it or not, are becoming appendages of their inventions, de-poeticizing the world around them?

But we have to live in that world. So we search, even there, for a new lyricism, like that of Saint-Exupéry, Ray Bradbury,

Richard Bach . . . And to preserve our individuality we turn back to childhood, as though to a golden age. "Where am I from? I'm from my childhood," says the author of *The Little Prince*. We return to the days of spring, when those five scouts were so busy! And in doing so, we look, listen, touch, smell, and taste with our souls. We enter that seemingly unreal world, which is actually real because it lives within us. It is natural and not of human making. This world is the time that has become our time, the time of our lives . . . It is us.

To Ivan Bunin's "In my heart I remember only my child-hood; nothing else belongs to me," Seneca would object: "Whatever is well said by anyone is mine."[6] After all, the reason a writer says anything is so that it can belong to others who are receptive to it. And Bunin, in the end, contradicts himself: In the poem "Evening,"[7] echoing Virgil in "Georgics" (II, 458),[8] he says that "happiness is just for those who know" and know-ing comes from others . . .

And as for happiness—albeit with a sad smile—what is it if not our apprehension of the world of things, by the mind and by the heart? What is it if not the comprehension of what we see and hear, of what we know, if not the realization that we're improving and that our souls are enriched, that everything is within us and up to us, that we can share our happiness with others, so that it multiplies and spreads—for both ourselves and other people?

"Carpe Diem"

_____

Do not inquire (we are not allowed to know) what end the gods have assigned to you and what to me, Leuconoe, and do not meddle with Babylonian horoscopes. How much better to endure whatever it proves to be, whether Jupiter has granted us more winters, or this is the last that now wears out the Etruscan Sea against cliffs of pumice. Take my advice, strain the wine and cut back far-reaching hopes to within a small space. As we talk, grudging time will have run on. Pluck the day, trusting as little as possible in tomorrow.[9]

It means something different to each person, that concise two-word phrase "Carpe diem!"* Initially, however, it belonged to two people alone, to _him_ and to _her_. Primarily to the woman, since the phrase was addressed to her. The voice of the choppy winter sea was also present. In short, monotone waves, it lashed the coastal cliffs, eroded by the eternal battle of two opposed elements: impetuous sea and immovable stone.

_____

* Usually translated as "Seize the day," the phrase "Carpe diem" from Horace's Ode 1.11 (also known as "To Leuconoe") has become a well-known aphorism. Its metrical foot is a choriamb, a combination of a trochee followed by an iamb (long-short-short-long or – ‿ ‿ –).

There was wine, too. Nothing costly—just the ordinary variety that he used to enjoy with close friends at his Sabine country home. He brought some along to his modest, cozy villa on the coast of the Tyrrhenian Sea, when he went there in the days before winter. It's believed that the Etruscans, that extraordinary people, artistically inclined and prone to dissipation, arrived in Italy by that very sea. But the Tyrrhenian Sea (also called the Etruscan) kept quiet about this and stood fast, ebbing and flowing, measuring the incessant passing of time in short, insistent choriambs: the trochee streaming onto the rocks and the iamb back out . . . And so, never breaking the rhythm or falling out of step, the sea hinted at something, called something to mind, and reached out to someone. Now, as it had for eternity . . .

And the man listened. What an abundance of sounds he carried within himself! From the barely audible whisper of leaves, the language of trees, and a creek's murmur to a crowd's roar at a performance. That's why, so often, his songs began with the question "Do you hear?" For he could hear what others failed to catch, whether a distant echo of someone's pipe or the voice of his own soul, which roused him when his attention waned. "Do you hear?" And he listened . . . He liked to listen, to listen closely and weave his poems from the sounds he heard—this became his occupation, his world. As the powerful waves pounded, accentuating the immeasurable muteness of eternity and the fragility of human existence, he was swept, as if by a wave, with a sharp feeling of loneliness and dislocation in the immensity of time and space. At that moment—one of those fleeting moments that make up the tapestry of human life—he felt, just as sharply, the need for sensual unity, for spiritual closeness.

But she, apparently, didn't hear. The Tyrrhenian Sea failed to reach her with its choriambs. It failed because she wasn't there in the present moment, in those intervals of time marked by the sea, but instead inhabited an illusory and misleading "tomorrow" that might never come at all. She was concerned with what *would* be, with the fate the gods would send them, even consulting the Chaldean astrologers (plentiful in imperial Rome), who, calculating the location of the stars, could say something for sure. Meanwhile, she was so near that he could pass her a glass of Sabine wine without even rising from his *klinai*, and yet—still so far away! And not just from him. It felt like she was somewhere else, even when she was speaking—about those fortune-tellers who read the stars, about prophetic signs . . . Nor did he really hear her words. Disinclined to superstition, he wasn't even paying attention. Instead, he bid farewell to those rushed, temporal snippets, filled with nothing, that the sea counted off as they faded into obscurity—beyond the horizon. He held his glass and listened . . .

And then, as he listened intently, he realized that the sea too was calling out to her, again and again, in the same choriamb: Léuconoé ("lucid thought"), a name not only melodious to the soul, but dear to the mind. For what greater gift can the immortals offer a human being than light sent down from heaven, from the radiant ether? This light imparts clarity of thought, setting the soul in a brighter key. That day, however, Jupiter was stingy with light: Low clouds hovered above the sea, whose green waves kept rushing onto the shore, tightly rolled and shaggy with white foam, hitting like a heavy hammer against the cliffs . . . But there is another gift of light from

the gods that humans must cherish above all and not let fade—
a particle of the heavenly aura sown in the soul. Hence the
name "Lucid thought." And yet, despite that name, Leuconoe
directed her thoughts toward tomorrow, to that which was
hidden from humankind behind a dark cloud, to the great
Unknown. It shadowed her thoughts, which, deprived of light,
darkened her open brow beneath her upswept hair.

Listening both to her and to the voice of the sea, he
reflected once more on the affinity between his art, that of the
word, and music, the art so cherished by those songbirds the
Hellenes. Say a word, and it's gone, already off the map: flying
like time itself, in time itself, in that precious morsel of it, as
though in a crystal glass. Touch a string, and you give voice to
time, embellish that morsel, make it audible or even tangible,
add color to it . . . It's then, listening to a multitude of skillfully
woven and many-hued specks of time, that our hearts sense
the flow of time—*fuga temporum*—and comprehend the value
of that which is lost, which can't be recalled or brought back . . .

Just before disappearing, the low winter sun, large and
crimson, peered out from the veil of clouds, trimming them
with a scant border of chilly gold. Ebbing and flowing, the
Tyrrhenian Sea counted down that eternal and indefatigable
sun's approach to the horizon. A few more resonant chori-
ambs and it would duck into the seas—somewhere in the far
West—until the next day (for the sun, tomorrow would defi-
nitely come) . . . He took a little handmade strainer (with a
squiggly pattern of tiny holes that resembled the sea's curves
and undulations), packed it with snow and poured his usual
Sabine wine through it because, even in winter, he preferred
it cold: The taste was more delicate, the color more brilliant.

Then some more for her—strained, cold . . . Their lips touched the thin edges of their glasses . . . And the sun touched the distant horizon . . . Again, the wave's voice—"Cárpe diém!"—a trochee accompanied, like a mirror reflection, by an iamb. In the sea's voice, he also heard an echo of his own. Once uttered, the phrase soared into the distance, into eternity, leaving only its echo: "Carpe diem! Carpe diem! . . ."

Perhaps because of the sun sinking subtly yet decisively to the horizon, it seemed to him that the winter day—and really every day—was a priceless gift to humanity that must be plucked and tasted. Otherwise, it would drop: A precious gift from heaven would be wasted and the soul would be impoverished, enfeebled, like the body without the fruit of the earth . . .

The western sun was still sparkling in the cut-crystal glasses—a warm smile in the cold wine. And, in *his* soul, a song—perhaps, his best—was taking shape amidst the rhythms of the Asclepiad meter, manifesting itself in sound. He would go on to present this song to *her* who, in the end, heeded those choriambs and entered with him, their souls united, into that fleeting moment—a moment brimming with soft light from the melodious name that was so sweet to his ear: Leuconoe.

The Mitten

I was pulling off my mitten,
and suddenly—
my hands stopped.
A memory
grazed my heart.
(Ishikawa Takuboku)[10]

I was walking down a deserted alley, through the previous night's snow—deep and fluffy. A narrow foot trail that had sprung up since daybreak led past a gray brick wall. Overlooking it was a school building of the same gray color, whose square pediment clock had long-since gone still and was now missing its hands. Bunches of white-encrusted rowan berries hung above the wall like tilted glasses, filled to the brim with ice-cold burgundy wine. The sky's all-encompassing blue reached down to the shimmering—almost blinding—white snow, flowing transparently into the stream of the footpath. "Ti-ti, tyu-tyu," came the clocklike call of some little bird, foretelling the coming of spring. And this was the only audible sound (besides the snow squeaking under my feet)—a greeting to the day's early light and its resplendent clarity. Anything else that might shake the silence was muffled by fluffy, untouched snow . . .

Suddenly, on its sparkling white surface, I saw a woman's black mitten. I stood for a good minute, riveted by the striking contrast of matte darkness and radiant white. It seemed that I'd just heard another sound: the voice of that black leather mitten. It lay there wracked with cold, losing the last remaining warmth of a woman's hand. It looked like a helpless creature, about to freeze. I bent down to pick it up but held back: You shouldn't take things that don't belong to you, even if they are lost. And what would I even do with it? At the end of the alley, I took one last look at that spot where the mitten was lying—a black dot on white . . . Turning onto the sidewalk, I sped up. The silence, syncopated with the snow's squeak, still drummed in my ears, filling up now with the city's rumble. The pristine white churned into brown porridge beneath my feet. Dulled by the rumble, the dazzling sunny morning and the lost mitten receded deep into my memory—humdrum and daily troubles prevailed.

Then I caught sight of a woman, strolling in front of me. She held a small purse, and also a mitten. A single mitten. I guessed right away that this woman had just walked down the same alley that I had. But she hadn't yet realized that she'd lost her mitten. I slowed down involuntarily. Hesitated. Should I let her know? What if the mitten were no longer there? Perhaps someone picked it up? Should I go back for it myself? But I couldn't very well say to a stranger: "just wait for me here." With each step, the idea of intervening became more ridiculous. Was it even her mitten lying in the snow? Dismissing the obvious answer, I tried to reassure myself and justify my indecision. Then picking up my pace again, I overtook the woman. As I passed, I stole a quick glance at her face. She was thinking her own thoughts, smiling faintly at someone in her mind.

Since then, I've often walked that winter path—both in my thoughts and in reality—alongside the gray brick wall, above which bunches of frost-encrusted rowan berries glow red, as though in crystal glasses. My eyes are blinded by the frigid, shimmering snow. And every time, I seem to catch sight of that crumpled mitten and imagine overtaking its owner who, despite being on the street, is nonetheless also in a different place, a different time, smiling at someone—someone known only to her. In my mind, I pick up the mitten so that later I can approach the stranger and return the lost object. I even hear my voice: "This isn't yours, is it?" I see the face of the woman, whose thoughts I've intruded upon: First she's confused but a moment later beams with joy at recovering a lost possession. My eyes keep following the two figures that for a little while still walk side by side. Then they part ways and take separate paths, vanishing into the city crowds. This image appears so vividly before my eyes that I sometimes feel a sense of calm: Maybe that's what actually happened. Maybe I did in fact return the woman's mitten, for the line between reality and fantasy is so tenuous.

The ancients professed that "an opportune moment is fleeting."[11] And indeed, one can never step in the same river twice. So I catch myself thinking that this isn't the same path as before. Nor is this the same blue sky streaming into it. Nor is this the same snow squeaking beneath my feet. Nor are these the same sunbeams dancing on the snow; they emanate from the same sun, but it changes with every moment. Nor are these the same clusters of rowan berries glowing red above the alley's gray brick wall, nor do they glisten with the same frosty juice. That's not the same little bird, announcing in eternal cadences the coming of some other, new spring. Even that school clock without hands flows with the current of time. And I myself am not the person I used to be. Only the heart's memory, a delicate thread that binds us to eternity, tries to recover the unrecoverable—the fleeting moment with its mood, colors, and sounds. Memory that by some arcane law tends to send important things spinning beyond its boundaries into oblivion, while fervently cherishing something insignificant and accidental. Like a woman's mitten, black on the blinding white snow . . .

A Room without Shadows

Once, on New Year's Eve, when large fluffy snowflakes began falling thick and fast as though to order, I went out, as always at that time, to wander the streets of old Lviv. I turned down a narrow lane, which, unexpectedly, was deserted despite its central location. Everything there appeared unalterable, embossed on the ages, like the dedication etched on the stone body of a building or monument. It seemed that the narrowness of that street had always been subsumed by thick fluffy snow—from before the beginning of time, as it would be forever, so long as the world existed. And there'd be no end to the abundant snowfall nor to the cosmic silence it underscored.

As I walked, I glanced up inadvertently at the illuminated windows. From the corner of my eye—into an unfamiliar world concealed from outside glances. Behind patterned curtains, flowered voile, and heavy drapes—only vague shapes and blurry orbs of yellowish, green, and pink light from desk and floor lamps . . . As many different worlds as windows. All on its own, the mind will creep behind what's hidden from the eye, painting a picture of cozy domesticity and of those enjoying it (who are not in the habit of roaming the city streets just before New Year's) . . .

Suddenly, I stopped. There before me was a bare window without even the sheerest covering, and in an instant I took in the whole room: It was lit by a bright incandescent bulb dangling from the ceiling on a long wire. In the middle of the room, on a little stool directly under that light, sat an old woman, wrapped in some dark garment, her head covered by a dark kerchief. Hunched low over a bucket, she was peeling potatoes. On the floor in a corner by the bed was a pile of stuff—old clothes. Nothing else and no one else. Not even a shadow or a shade of color: the naked bulb flooded the barren room with a blinding, and in no way cozy, light . . .

I couldn't see the woman's face: It was hidden by the kerchief, which had fallen down over her forehead. Nor was there anything to look at in the room. Time slipped away from me, and I stood there mesmerized; something wouldn't let me step away from the window . . . And the snow kept falling, even more quickly and heavily in the strip of bright light emanating from that uncovered window. And it seemed like the snow was falling not only outside the window but there, inside the room, landing heavily on the shoulders of that solitary woman.

There was nothing to break my trance. Not a soul turned onto the street to make me feel embarrassed by my curiosity. Nor did it appear that the woman would ever raise her dejected eyes . . . Also, it seemed to me that not only had the snow's unvaried descent and the unearthly silence always existed, but that they would continue eternally in the narrowness of that desolate street. So too would the woman in the uncovered window always remain hunched over her potatoes, as though locked in endless contemplation . . .

And so it was. It's been a long time since I've roamed the streets of old Lviv on New Year's Eve: The sweet anticipation of something new and unusual no longer caresses my soul, not even in dreams, nor when evening snowfall paints over the gray monotony of everyday life. But as soon as the last day of December dwindles to a close, it's like I'm standing, as I once did, long ago, on deserted Staroievreiska Street in front of that uncovered window. I see the same relentless snowfall, heavy on the shoulders of that recluse, all wrapped up in dark clothing, hunched over her potatoes in the middle of an empty room without even a shadow beside her.

The Silver-Haired Wind

Gusting at autumn's doorstep, an itinerant wind flips the pages of books laid out for sale on the square, directly on the concrete slabs by the monument to The Printer, Ivan Fedorov, a Ukrainian Gutenberg.[12] It turns the leaves so hastily and impatiently that they shimmer. Then suddenly it takes an interest and settles on a certain page, calming down.

Passing the square, I too stopped before the rustling pages, to take a closer look—What's the autumn wind reading? Books from my distant youth: *A Journey to the Sea, The Bread of Those Early Years, Sunlight on Cold Water, And Never Said a Word*.[13] Pages yellowed . . .

Glancing through their titles, I suddenly remembered another wind, also in early autumn, that touched not only my face, but my soul. This wind had visited the square some thirty years earlier, when there'd been no bronze monument to Ivan Fedorov, and no book market, either.

Different. That wind was different—silver-haired. Perhaps because the trees, swaying in the wind, glistened with silver. And the air, too, on that misty September day, was made silvery by the wind—not blustery, but flowing in a single, steady, noise-filled current. And I was tempted to yield to that current and stream along with it: to flow with the wind, into the wind . . .

It too was flipping pages . . . I don't know what book it was. It lay open in the lap of a girl sitting on a bench in a little park. The wind flipped the pages unhurriedly, one at a time, and they trembled gently, as though beneath a tender touch.

The square and the little park were deserted at the time. The girl, I noticed from afar, wasn't the one reading—it was the wind that was turning the pages. She was riveted by the silver-gray of that September afternoon.

Our eyes met, but only for the brief, trivial moment when I was passing her bench. The most I could do was slow down. I couldn't even conceive of stopping. I couldn't think of a single word I'd say to the girl: No matter what I said, it would be inappropriate, it would brutally rip the fine fabric of the wind, destroying it completely. Only a moment's glance could coexist with this mood that the wind had blown in; anything else would disturb it and scare it off.

After a minute or two, I crossed the street and looked around. The wind was still flipping the pages of a book whose title I would never know. Nor would I ever learn the name of the girl who, on that distant autumn day, sensed the exceptional energy of that wondrous September wind, her soul united with mine.

And now when each year is newly touched by autumn, I listen for the wind's voice. I go to that square where it flips, hastily or unhurriedly, through books that few people care about nowadays. And sometimes I get the feeling that someone is talking to me, no longer from rustling pages—from leaves of paper—but from the massive worldwide web with words illuminated on a monitor, and that this someone is speaking with me about the loneliness of silver-haired wind.

In the Language of Rain

___

Il pleut doucement sur la ville.
(Arthur Rimbaud)[14]

Sometimes I feel as though I understand the language of rain, at least its Lviv dialect, when it rains quietly on the city—a quiet that would be nearly inaudible, were it not met by the roofs of *kamyanytsias* and the leaves of trees and by the sensitive membranes of umbrellas. Straining for all they're worth, umbrellas relay the language drizzling over the city, capturing the rain's whisper: plip-plop, plip-plop ... And it's not so much with the ear but with the soul that we heed this whisper, its lilt, when, for no reason, we step out the door beneath an open umbrella and listen to the language of rain, spend time with it, when it rains quietly on the city ...

It's something special, that space beneath the umbrella, delicately defined by droplets. The most modest of nomadic dwellings, the umbrella squires its recluse-tenant through the rainy city's streets and squares; its illusory coziness encourages contemplation, spinning some private thought or creating a particular mood in unison with the rain's whisper. And since thought, as the ancients observed, is marked by action, by what one does, I unwittingly enlist the rain in my struggles with translation: When it's drizzling quietly on the town / Verlaine's translator puzzles over tone / his grief in the day-to-day is sewn / When it's drizzling quietly on the town / No matter how he twists the words around / The poem's languor piercing through the soul / finds no expression, no parole / No matter how he twists the words around . . . / The rain falls quietly, in its lonely patter / In the footsteps of Verlaine's autumn song / The hour is late, the day is gone / The rain falls quietly, in its lonely patter . . .

And so, at least it seems to me, I sometimes start to understand the language of rain. When it rains very quietly, impersonally (for the phrase is subjectless, after all) and when, in a blur of space and time, the usual "here and now" loses its reality—it's then that from the rain's monotone whisper, intercepted by the umbrella, a message comes through. The quieter it is, the more distinctly I hear it: "No i cóż dalej, szary człowieku?"* That whispered voice takes me back to the Bernardine monastery,[15] to the Historical Archive once housed there, which I remember especially because of the view from its windows—onto rainy, mist-veiled Lviv. On rainy days, dense shadows gathered there behind the massive gray walls, and a glaring 100-watt bulb burned all day in a chandelier hanging from the vaulted Gothic ceiling. Illuminating the Records Room with its dispersed smell of antiquity, also gray, that permeated the parchment and paper documents, it drove the vague shadows of the past into the corners.

I heard the question from the lips of Valentyna Kornylivna Siverska,[16] a short, slight woman employed in the Department of Historical Records who, after years of singing in Lviv's Trembita[17] choir, tasted the bitterness of lost hope, forced separation, and loneliness and gave herself over to archival

---

* "So what's next, then, my gray man?" (Polish).

antiquity, spending all her days in the archives. She probably would have spent her nights there too, if she'd been allowed. I can still see her in her archival "uniform," a quilted jacket, a faded blue smock, and felt boots (the subterranean depositories were cold and damp even in the summer), with a smile lightly sketched on her thin, bloodless lips. Her sorrowful, though not altogether humorless, archival smile was the natural setting for a reverberation or snippet of the rain's question "Cóż dalej?"—What's next?

I've stopped trying to capture that question in Ukrainian (more pesky problems of translation!): It will never be quite the same, and not only because a translation "whispers" differently than the original. The crucial untranslatable part is "szary człowiek," which in no way corresponds to *sira liudyna chy cholovik*, gray person or man, in Ukrainian: The warm irony of the Polish question—one "gray man" to another—here becomes condescending. "Cóż dalej?" is a rhetorical question, for what could possibly come next when there's no time or space, just grayness all around? The question is really a greeting, used when two kindred spirits meet, or a pass-phrase that makes it possible to recognize one's own kind—a peer, with whom one feels glad, not only to share a few words, but a silence. "I'm nobody! Who are you? / Are you nobody, too? / Then there's a pair of us—don't tell! / They'd banish us, you know."[18] These verses from Emily Dickinson weren't on Valentyna Kornylivna's lips but in her expression, when she addressed me with that soft "Cóż dalej?" so redolent of the language of rain.

When, on an overcast day, picking up on and interpreting the rain's whisper, I wander down some deserted street where there's no rumble of cars, no pedestrian noise, the question sounds so clearly beneath the umbrella's canopy that I sometimes turn to look: Perhaps someone has entered my tiny dwelling, parting the ribbons of rain? But a moment later I realize: It wasn't a person on the street, or even the rain, but the all-encompassing grayness, which lifts the weight of centuries-old Gothic structures from the shoulders of the Atlantes and Caryatids and smooths the scars on the bodies of stone buildings, so that the whole city feels lighter and one's soul is eased. It's that very grayness speaking to me, in the language of the rain when it falls softly on the city.

The Felled Shadow

Leñador.
Córtame la sombra.
(Federico García Lorca)

Woodcutter,
cut down my shadow![19]

It inscribed itself on the ground, even at night as soon as the streets only lamp went on—the shadow of a shriveled black locust. The street was really just a narrow path running between a brick wall, behind which a long-neglected garden belonging to no one lived out its last days, and a schoolyard fence. The shriveled tree kept out of the schoolyard: It would just have been a hassle there. No one bothered to chop it down because it pressed close to the fence, and only the remnant of a once dense green crown lay upon the road as a bizarre shadow—a lattice of blackened twigs. What driver or pedestrian would honestly be troubled by the shadow of a dead tree?

The path was frequented by people out for a walk, usually as evening fell. They paid no attention to the dried-up tree, didn't hear its voice imprinted in the eccentric shadow beneath their feet. They walked, oblivious (mostly, starry-eyed lovers), up to Vysokyi Zamok Park to gaze at the city and to dream. I too used to walk that path, nearly every day, especially in the years when I was working at the Lviv Historical Archive. Locked from 9 to 6 in the depths of the Bernardine Monastery that housed the archives, I too longed to gaze at the city from above, at the monastery's tower, and at the sun drawing close to the horizon . . .

So, recalling my walks up to Vysokyi Zamok, I always see the shriveled locust tree this way: blackened and dried up. Only in springtime would some greenery appear here and there amidst its black branches. And when its scanty sap, that had miraculously risen through the dead wood, finally ran out, the tree eked out its life's (or death's?) last blossom, adding a smatter of white to its dry, meticulously inked crown. The intense white of the blossom was something incredible—the last spring fancy of the desiccated tree. From then on there was blackness and nothing else. But on certain winter days, when the sky cleared after a snowstorm and snow subtly accentuated every twig, every angle—white on black—the dry crown was enchanting, impressing its exquisite design, like a Japanese print, on the sky's frosty blue . . .

No matter how many times I looked at the shriveled black locust, at its shadow inscribed on the path, to me that shadow, the thing beneath my feet, was never the locust's voice—it was merely a reflection of the dead crown. Then, just when I was planning to quit my job at the archive, in the late 1960s, I came across García Lorca's "Song of the Barren Orange Tree," leafing through a newly purchased little volume of Mykola Lukash's translations. It was there that I discovered the tree's voice: "Woodcutter, cut down my shadow! / May I not be tormented, may I not see / myself in nakedness . . ." Since then, those two trees—the orange one somewhere in the scorching-hot lands of old Andalusia, and the shriveled black one on the doorstep of Vysokyi Zamok—have become entwined in my imagination.

"As if in punishment I'm placed / between mirrors. / The day distorts me as it wishes / The night taunts me with stars," continues the orange tree in Lukash's voice . . .[20] The shriveled black locust seemed to assist me in my musings on translation—especially with its shadow that I stepped upon. That shadow, in tandem with the sun's journey across the sky, with the day's march, seemed to circle the tree as if to say: "Just look what you've become . . ." "So the day doesn't actually 'distort the tree,'"—I challenged the Ukrainian translator in my mind—it walks around it ("El día me da vueltas"), whereas the night "replicates" the tree's angular desiccation in all its spiny stars ("Y la noche me copia / en todas sus estrellas") . . . "Woodcutter, cut down my *tin'* . . ." and in that Ukrainian noun *tin'*—for the Spanish *sombra*—I could hear the lightning blow of an ax—too quick even to produce an echo—into the flesh of a tree: *tin'*! . . .

And then it happened. Sometime in March, when the trees were still bare and their sap pushed upward to their crowns, a new day arrived at that little street, but there was no longer anything to circle—the day stumbled on a bare stump. At some point, I too stumbled there, but not on the stump—on the barren spot, like a chink in the sky. It occurred to me that I might have taken the wrong street. At first, I didn't grasp what was missing. Then I noticed the stump. Someone must have heard the voice of the black locust or, more likely, cut it down because its blackness was an eyesore. Today, not even a trace of that stump remains.

That day when I got home, wet, lumpy snowflakes suddenly clouded the sky, erasing everything from sight. But I do remember one thing: a butterfly beating its rainbow wings against the windowpane. Warmth must have lifted it up there that morning, while the afternoon snowstorm pinned it to the window. It was like a restless soul that could find no refuge . . .

Every now and then I still take that path to Vysokyi Zamok. But I don't always think of the black locust tree. Occasionally, though, when the path is dusted with snow, a mysterious design flashes suddenly on the backdrop of white; as if in dark cracks of lightning, that familiar felled shadow inscribes itself again.

The World between the Windowpanes

It leaves us, like so many other worlds—that glass-enclosed world between the windowpanes. It goes back where it came from—the world of childhood to which everyone, not only children, must bid farewell. It departs quietly, subtly, like a sunbeam fading on the windowpane at dusk. Like quaint flowers painted meticulously on the window by frost. Like a fairy tale, told every evening before prayer time. Like a song passed from a mother's soul to a child's. Like the cradle itself... "Saturn smoothly erases..."[21]

The world between the windowpanes is a world that belongs to the city or, more precisely, to its outskirts in whose very street names—Garden, Flower, Hay, Violet, Cherry—one can sense the countryside and see the horizon... A child doesn't even need to stand on tiptoes to peer into this world, which appears in the low windows of one- or two-story *kamyanytsias*, modest little homes. It is an in-between world because it belongs neither to the interior nor to the exterior, though the multitudinous toy figures that have taken refuge there all turn to face the street. So do the cards with images of saints and every imaginable kind of potted plant: anything that strives and climbs upward, blossoming in a plethora of colors, as well as other plants that bloom only in dreams or fairy tales—after all, thick green ferns harboring the memory of lush primeval forests also reside between the window-panes. Time is measured differently there: Christmas decorations arranged on cotton-wool snow may sit around until Easter, when they'll get acquainted with the *pysanky*, elaborately painted eggs. And only a few tiny specks of dust that have made their way into that space between the panes remind us of the seasons' relentless passing, of the monotonous gray weekdays that trudge by noiselessly, on both sides of the glass . . .

We can set forth anytime for the city's outskirts, toward the cozy world between the windowpanes. But we rarely chance to touch or enter that world (averse to both commotion and bright lights) unless it itself calls out to a passerby. This may happen on a Sunday or a holiday, at the crack of dawn, when the outskirts are tranquil—particularly quiet and deserted, when this silence is accented by the faintest drizzle that barely dusts the glass rather than scattering it with tears, touching the soul more than the face. It is precisely at this time, when the streets and homes haven't yet come to life, that the world between the windowpanes may open itself to a lonely passerby, who's stepped out with no purpose, following its voice into the quiet morning drizzle.

At this point, it's time to describe the special mood in which we enter that extraordinary world that connects the houses and the streets, and so I recall the ancients who referred to language or, more precisely, to the tongue, as the translator of the soul (*lingua interpres animi*): How can we translate what lies beyond the word? I also think of Pascal, staring at the tip of his quill: "A thought has escaped me. I would write it down. I write instead that it has escaped me."[22] Today's writers stare at their monitors, and if they reflect on their writing for too long or just stop and let their thoughts wander, their screens start to dim and sparkle coldly. They become the image of a cosmic gap in which points of light rush at tremendous speeds and vanish into black infinity—uncharted and incalculable, worlds and worlds beyond. Returning to Pascal: "The eternal silence of these infinite spaces alarms me."[23]

The world between the windowpanes is a world opposed to cosmic silence and to the bustle of the city, where, despite its jostling, there is so much loneliness and so little warmth or comfort. Building that world between the windowpanes, a child's hand unwittingly returns what the city takes from its inhabitants: A path to oneself, to childhood, to one's village, where everything, from a wildflower to the stars above, is endowed with a soul and language—a singsong language replete with diminutives and terms of endearment. Encased in fragile glass, the world between the windowpanes is a kind of refuge for those diminutives, for that kindness . . .

So, the path to the world between the windowpanes is the path to oneself, difficult to take (for we're always in such a hurry), but even when taken, rarely followed to the end. I recall my strolls in Zamarstyniv on the outskirts of Lviv as something distant and inaccessible: the little mist-shrouded vegetable patches crouched before old homes, the low windows shielded by cheap translucent curtains, the silence of the sleepy rooms behind them . . . Except that behind one of those windows, I remember a piano echoing the faint drizzle, always the same chords—time after time someone would play the monotonous tune "Dzień jak co dzień."[24] "A day like any other," the song goes, "a typical day, like any other" . . . Typical in every way, without change or novelty, an ordinary day fallen silent, the kind of day when the world between the window-panes begins to speak . . . As I said, I recall this as something distant and inaccessible, though the city's outskirts are easily reached: Just wait for the green light at the intersection and cross the main road . . .

"Now look—my infancy is long ago, dead: and I am alive," St. Augustine writes in his *Confessions*.[25] Sometimes, even if only in my mind, I nevertheless dare to cross that main road packed with cars. I wander through the tangle of quiet streets and alleys. But I can't find the world between the window-panes. Instead, I see my own reflection in modern plexiglass windows where there's just one pane and no room for that world. It is then that I hear the voice that so often haunts me. It is all of classical antiquity, not just Seneca, trying to break through not only to a lonely individual headed somewhere in a hurry, but to all of humanity, with the words, as extraordinary as the world between the windowpanes: "Hasten to find me, but hasten to find yourself first"[26] . . .

The Owl

———————

Back in my youth, when I was renting various places, I never lucked into a mansard room. Once, however, I came across a small room (on Lysenko Street), directly beneath the roof; its windows looked out on the wooded slopes of Kaiserwald and beyond them, the flatlands outside the city. But for some reason that I no longer even remember, I never moved into that roof-enclosed nook. Since then, I've gotten into the habit not only of observing mansard windows, but of listening to them when they're illuminated at night—Gothic, Romanesque, Baroque. As soon as Evening takes to his conductor's stand, a flickering scale reverberates in the stone symphony of the old town, from the lowest *Do*, like the sound of a squat gate on Virmenska Street, to the highest *La*, hit by the Gothic windows on Kniazia Romana Street where, as in Paul Verlaine, "The sky is breathing down upon the roof"[27] . . .

But most often, in the depths of my memory, I hear the windows that never lit up—not mansard windows, but attic ones, and not in the city, but in my father's home in Vyriv. This was an old brick house inhabited by a succession of village priests and their families. I guess I must have done less damage to the stairs of my current place than to those old stairs that I've shuffled up countless times in my thoughts. But do steps taken in one's mind have any weight at all? Is it possible to wear down that which no longer exists? The parish office was long ago converted into a school and from the old building only the brick walls were kept. Now there's no trace of those, either: On the same lot, someone is building themselves a house. And though it no longer exists, I still climb the wooden staircase from the dusky entrance hall to the attic. I walk on the inner edges of the stairs, right against the wall, afraid they'll creak under my childish feet. But why childish? In fact, I don't know who it is that climbs the stairs to the attic several times per day. Is it a little boy or a man burdened by time? Or maybe the little boy leads the gray-haired man by the hand? He leads apprehensively but with a childish determination, day after day, step after step. That must be it.

But then, one stifling summer day long ago, I climbed the stairs all alone. It was as though I'd gradually surfaced from one world into a completely different one, and all the mystery, all the magnetism of that world was contained in a single short word—attic—that, in my mind, reverberated with "panic." I got a whiff of this world about halfway up the stairs—the incomparable aroma of objects abandoned to time. Thickly layered, stratum upon strata, was everything that, having been acquired by human hands, and having served that person, finally fell out of use. A homeowner picks up such an object that's really just in the way ("Though it might still come in handy sometime . . .") and moves it to the attic.

But, in fact, these types of practical considerations rarely decide an object's fate. We don't lay hands on something that's been a friend—through work and relaxation, joy and sorrow, weekdays and holidays—and simply toss it to the wind. And this is why layers of abandoned objects agglomerate in the attic. To take account of them or just to sort them would be one of those incredible feats that is recounted only in fairy tales.

In the middle of it all, like a boat that has survived miraculously intact through a terrible shipwreck, is an ash-wood cradle, suspended from the rafters. Listing and leaning in the attic's shoreless expanses, it's on the verge of sinking, dissolving in the deluge of things. The eye finds nothing to rest upon. Objects upon objects—large and small, wooden and metal, ceramic and clay, wicker and woven . . . but it's hopeless. We can't begin to sort them using such categories—not by size and shape, nor by material.

There we find a quaint sooty-paned iron lantern from centuries past (it was once attached to a carriage), broken fauteuils with springs, poking out from rotten fabric, parasols, and all kinds of toys. There too are the remnants of objects whose purpose we can no longer guess. When we bend down and rummage through them, these incredible things beg to be held, speaking up from that massive junkyard: a little whirligig on a carved stem that once turned beneath a glass cupola in the sun; a luxurious and artistic piece of ironwork—the frame of a tabletop oil lamp adorned with griffins; a large tasseled lampshade for a hanging (salón-style) lamp of a stiff, formerly sun-yellow fabric; a broken hourglass and a nonfunctional clock (the one with no sand, the other—with no hands) . . . People's every day, every night companions. Objects that gave forth their voices: shining, moving, comforting, helping, measuring the march of hours and minutes, and transporting us to the world of fairytales. Things that now seem to amount to nothing, but are still immeasurably more dear to us than new ones. More dear, because of the souls that people have breathed into them. New things can't die because there's no life in them yet.

So anyway, about halfway up the stairs I was already sensing the attic's incomparable aura—of objects abandoned there. It was scorching-hot outside. Heat emanated from the tin roof, and the breath of bygone days was especially pronounced. This time, finding myself in the attic, I decided to make the rounds, starting in the middle, where the cradle hung. Once fiery orange, but now discolored and covered in cobwebs, the cradle, like everything around it, had acquired an ashy hue that in the sunlight looked silver.

I was searching for somewhere to step, when I suddenly froze in place with my foot lifted. Right where I'd been planning to put it down, right there, stretching out, or so it seemed to me, its vast copper wings, lay a motionless owl. A silver strip of sunlight, saturated with the finest dust and penetrating through the attic window, thrust itself directly into it. The owl had dived head-first amidst the things, while seeming to shield them with its wings, protecting them from gawking eyes, or from relentless and ubiquitous decay, which nothing ever outlives. A second slower, and I would have stepped on the owl. But even then, it wouldn't have moved, for it was dead. It shared the fate of countless other things in the attic and had itself become an object.

Since then—after more than half a century!—the image of the owl has stuck stubbornly in my memory. And never mind my memory, it's in my soul. Sometimes when I'm walking, a broad maple leaf lands at my feet and I shudder—I see that owl again. I still don't fully understand why it gave me such a fright back then. It was immediately clear that it was dead and incapable of any harm. But now I realize the true cause of my fear. I was struck by something completely irreconcilable: the bird's vigilance, on the one hand, and its unflappability in such close proximity to a human. Someone could pick it up, examine it, like any other object in the attic, and it wouldn't stir. But I'd never do such a thing because I knew that the owl, unlike all those other things, brought to life only in our imaginations, had once really been alive. I was horrified seeing that which was opposite to life.

But even in death, the owl had struck me as somehow special—unlike other birds. It didn't steal away into some dark corner, but fell smack in the middle of the attic, wings spread, as though desiring to take under its protection as many of the abandoned things as possible. It mostly likely fell at night, though it could still see everything around it keenly. For Night herself, divine mother of Death and Sleep, was selected by the owl, not only for flight, but for its eventual fall. It fell, releasing, perhaps, a barely audible sigh—aww-uhhh— and echoing its name, as breathtaking as the bird itself.

So when on a gusty autumn day a red leaf falls rapidly and noiselessly at my feet, I start back in fright: That owl is everywhere, even there on the sidewalk. And when leaves take to the air in a sudden windstorm, flapping in the darkened sky, it seems to me that the nocturnal bird has just plummeted into the dark socket of some neglected mansard—aww-uhhh . . .

At the Intersection

Through the window of a city bus, early in the morning, when rush hour is at its worst, a snapshot of your face. Its expression— contemplative or simply blank, like a passenger's—didn't change because the moment was so short, just a tremor in time (it happens sometimes that, spotting a familiar face in oncoming traffic, we don't recognize it right away, but an instant later, from a snapshot we've saved in our memory). Nor did I manage to react with a smile or a wave. A little while later, you smiled and waved (a motion in motion). But that was already in my imagination as, using a thread of moments, buses and cars wove and wove the shifting and resounding meshwork of everyday life. And perhaps, too, in your imagination, I smiled and greeted you with a wave . . .

We kept looking at each other in this manner, exchanging smiles, happy to have met that morning, although we were already far apart. But were we really? By "we," I don't mean the ones between whom, at that early hour, the distance was rapidly increasing. I mean the "we" that stayed behind: you with me and I with you. In this version of "us," we lived strange lives independent of ourselves: I within you, and you within me.

At a distant intersection, tearing through the ever-expanding meshwork of an ordinary morning, a traffic light briefly turned red. Rumbling—then everything silent; motion— then everything still. I stepped onto the white-striped crosswalk when the light turned green. As I crossed, you kept waving at me from that wondrous snapshot (it persisted in my memory). Maybe it was you, or maybe it was the fleeting moment itself, which we'd managed to snatch from the rush of traffic . . . This salvaged moment is priceless, / for time is an echo of loss: It is us.[28]

The Whirligig

No one remembers when he first appeared here—the man with the whirligig in his hands. It must have been long ago, since everyone has grown used to him, as one grows used to a lamppost, a pole, or anything on the street: They pay no attention and just pass by.

In any case, there's no need to avoid the man with the whirligig, for he never bothers anyone. He sits on the stone foundation wall of a wrought-iron fence, right on the corner, never without his whirligig—a propeller planed from a piece of wood, spinning on a nail and mounted on a long pole. There he is regardless of the weather—hot or cold—dressed identically for all seasons in a worn padded jacket, threadbare pants, a hat with earflaps, and thick boots.

Over time, all of his clothing has turned as gray as the wall on which he sits, as the pavement, as the sidewalk, and as the apartment buildings with their peeling, mud-spattered plaster. No one notices him or speaks a word to him. Except maybe a street sweeper who, collecting fallen leaves and chestnut shells on the sidewalk, rustling his broom past the wizened boots of the man with the whirligig, happens to call out to him, for want of anything else to do:

"So, how are things, Ladzio? Turning?"

Or when it's calm out and neither the whirligig nor a single leaf flutters:

"So what's up, Ladzio? Nothing turning?"

Ladzio doesn't answer. Probably doesn't hear—he stares fixedly in one direction, as though expecting someone.

No one notices him, nor does he notice anyone. And what is there to attract anyone's attention? Not many people in this corner of the city and even less commotion. Only occasionally, when the weather's warm, and bottled beer is brought to the kiosk across the street, does excitement reign for a time. Those wishing to refresh themselves with an intoxicating beverage storm the kiosk. They drink straight from the bottle, throwing their heads back. From afar, it looks like they're blowing into trumpets, but the sound is inaudible. When their thirst is quenched, they scatter.

Ladzio pays no attention to them, not when they're drinking, nor as they scatter, lighting cigarettes and cracking jokes. He holds up his whirligig to catch a stray wind that's wandered down the alley—so intent, as though engaged in God knows what kind of solemn act.

Behind Ladzio and behind the wall upon which he sits is an abandoned stadium. Every day, at the same hour of the afternoon, an elderly couple—husband and wife, or maybe old friends—strolls along the track. Trudging after them, maintaining a respectful distance—not too near and not too far—is a little short-legged dog . . . "But when we were young . . ." The dog stops, for he's heard this phrase before: Anticipating a prolonged pause in the walk, he sits down.

Ladzio doesn't see this because he never looks behind him. He holds the handle of his whirligig, clamped between his palms. When it's windy, the pole trembles, as though alive. So long as the wind is there between his palms, the whirligig turns, and that means that everything on earth is following its course—it's all turning.

Now a bus will pass. Only this event draws Ladzio's attention. The old bus, meandering through the maze of suburban streets, shows up here every half hour. As soon as it peers around the corner, Ladzio comes to life, preparing to meet it. Aloft, like a battle flag, he hoists his whirligig. He listens for its rattle, ever more sensitive to the pole's subtle quiver that he catches with his palms. And when there's a stiff wind, when the rattling doesn't let up, even for a moment, Ladzio's eyes shine with exultation, as though to say: "See here! The wind! It's in my hands! I'm holding it! Look!"

The bus creaks, lulling its passengers to sleep. As it bounces over a pothole, all nod their heads as though unanimously affirming Ladzio's joy. Then they doze off again, plunge into sleep, thinking their thoughts—neither sad nor happy. No one looks out the bus's window, at the street. Only the driver stays awake, watching the same bumpy road, the same old gray before him . . . A minute later, the bus vanishes around a turn. Fallen leaves, newspaper scraps, and all sorts of trash swirl up in its wake. As the street empties out again, it plunges back into drowsing, into the aroma of roasted barley coffee that wafts around these parts, in the Zamarstyniv district (there's a roastery nearby). And only the whirligig high above Ladzio's head catches the rustle of autumn that flies in from the nearby slopes of Vysokyi Zamok, already blushing red . . .

No one knows when he first sat down on that stone wall at the base of the iron fence with the whirligig in his hands. And no one notices when, for the first time one windy late autumn day, he isn't there. Except for the street sweeper who, collecting wind-tossed leaves with his broom and approaching the spot where Ladzio always sat, is on the verge of asking:

"So, how are things, Ladzio? Turning?"

But not seeing the old kersey boots in their usual spot, he says to himself: "Whirligig's gone. Too bad. It would be spinning like mad today. What a mean wind is blowing!"

Praesens Historicum

To be sure, history is not that which was and is no more, but rather something we live, or at least should live: "Those who do not live with the past do not live at all," an ancient thinker once asserted...

Every scorching August, when the Lviv cobblestones breathe fire underfoot as though possessed by the heat, when ailing chestnuts rustle, my thoughts return to the year 1518, to a summer day, to an hour and moment described in stern Latin by Józef Zimorowicz in the Lviv chronicle:

> Tot cladibus caelitus immissis concussa Leopolis, ne maiorem Nemesim flagitiis impunitis in ultionem sui accenderet, Iwaszkonem Armenum et Sophiam Christianam ob prolern secum susceptam, tanquam sacrilegis amplexibus religionem polluissent, ad rogum damnavit. Trahebantur extra portam uterque uno compede vincti, bardocucullis carbaseis, pice resinaque illitis, ad talos induti, facibus feralibus, igne incesto scintillantibus, manus armati, quibus primo pyram, mox sese succenderunt, nequiquam lacrimis ultrices flammas exstinguere conantes, frustra et Armenis ad eiulatum contribulis sui eminus quiritantibus.

When Lviv was struck by so many calami-
ties from on high for the unpunished sins
of Iwaszko the Armenian and Sophia the
Christian, who carried his child—those who
had desecrated the faith with their wicked
embraces—the city sentenced them to burn-
ing at the stake so as not to unleash upon itself
the rage of Nemesis. They were bound by a
single rope and dragged outside the city gate,
then wrapped from head to toe in linen vest-
ments soaked in tar and resin. They were made
to hold infernal torches sputtering with illicit
fire, which first they used to light the pyre, and
then themselves, trying in vain to extinguish
the vengeful flames with their tears. And from
afar, Armenians responded in vain to the cries
of their countryman with a loud lament . . .

Of the misfortunes that preceded the execution, one was a
mighty summer flood some years earlier . . . "of the rather feeble
Poltva River. Fed by constant rains and by the waters of neigh-
boring ponds, it suddenly became so swollen that it surged
through ditches, walls, and canals. Torn from their foundations
on the outskirts of the city, houses bobbed about in its swells.
To reach the St. Stanislaus *kościół*, transformed as it was into
a waterlogged island, required the use of an oar or a sail." And
then, only a month after the flood, the Tatars invaded: "Having
suddenly taken over all of Ruthenian lands, they descended
upon Lviv like a heavy cloud, doing so on St. Anna's Day . . ."

It's difficult to know whether the chronicle's author derived these gory details of Zosia and Iwaszko's execution from oral accounts or from written sources; it's not impossible that it was from the former, since he was born in Lviv on the 20th of August 1597, less than eighty years after the couple was led to their death. A man of his time, he detailed the gruesome scene in the spirit of that time—without the slightest shadow of sympathy for the unlucky pair. Yet, perhaps concealed behind his allusions to Nemesis—goddess of human fate, who looks after the social order and personifies divine punishment—and behind all the traditional locutions borrowed from ancient poetry (specifically, about the appeal of "illicit love affairs," *incestos amores*, from Horace's *Odes*;[29] about the "flame of revenge," *ultrix flamma* from Virgil's *Aeneid*[30]) lay some fleeting shadow of sympathy for those two, sentenced to death by burning, and not only for the two of them (for "... she carried his child")—perhaps ... As for Matviy Seles from Drohobych, "a well-known lawyer and municipal syndic," it's unlikely he felt the slightest shadow of pity, since he served as prosecutor in the case against Iwaszko the Armenian and Sophia the Christian: he was the one who secured their sentence of burning at the stake. But who knows; maybe belatedly, in his sleep or in his dying hour (in the year 1532), scorching drops of remorse—to paraphrase Aeschylus—fell upon him from obscurity, who knows ...

Writing in the style of the high classics about the "flame of revenge" prepared for Zosia and Iwaszko, Zimorowicz could hardly have imagined that this locution would better describe a different conflagration—one that Nemesis, having waited nine years (*nonum in annum*, as the ancients, versed in numerology, would have said),[31] prepared for the city. "'Twas nine sum-mers after their death / on a scorching hot day at its zenith / A wailing wave of fire struck the city /Its mane of flames avenged the lovers / fought fire with fire and ire with ire / Though hard to believe, id factum est . . ."[32]

Id factum est: It happened. In that completed action, there is also a shade of the present tense: The "it" (*id*) happened, and therefore it is—*est* . . . The fire that raged in 1527, nine summers after Zosia and Iwaszko's incineration, burned down the entire city of Lviv and killed quite a few people, accord-ing to the chronicle. The wind, blew first one way, then the other, as though making sure that everything would be reduced to smoldering rubble. And "turning northward" (as D. Zubrytskyi writes), it snatched a flaming firebrand from the tower overlooking the Kraków Gates and carried it to Vysokyi Zamok, and farther still—to the Znesinnia district." Let's recall that the condemned couple was dragged *extra portam*, i.e., beyond the city gates—most likely these very Kraków Gates, historians believe. It was precisely in this quar-ter of the city that the devastating fire began to rage.

If so, the horrible event took place very near there, in a hol-low at the crossroads, where the Number 6 tram now turns on its way to the Lviv Opera House. Perhaps it was from that hill, where the Ukrainian Church of Our Lady of the Snows, for-merly a *kościół*, now stands, that Armenians lamented. Later they haughtily refused the monetary "reparations" that King Sigizmund ordered the Lviv municipal councilors to pay them after an appeal.

Hearing these laments in my mind, I accompany the con-demned couple as they step toward the pyre. But I never imagine the horrible scene that follows—so as not to reignite (the strange thought haunts me) the unfortunate pair's suffering. I think only of the fact that the somber participle *morituri*[33]—those who are about to die—a future active form that does not even exist in Ukrainian, doesn't even come close to capturing what the convicted pair felt.

And so, when Lviv sends forth its fiery breath, I step back to that strange time—the historical present. Whenever I pass the crossroads where Krakivska Street leads to the former Volynsky high road, amidst the rumble of cars, the jingling of trams, and the street's cacophony, among the fleeting shadows—of trees, stone buildings, and life itself, which in this city is so bustling and noisy—the voice of an elegiac poet reaches me by some miracle, despite the distance of more than two millennia: "The Blessed Dead exist. Death does not end it all; / A pale shadow escapes, defeating the pyre."[34] And it seems to me that these words, too, are about Zosia and Iwaszko. Except that, for the two lovers whose fates were entwined, the pyre was murderous before becoming ceremonial.

The Flute

In the depths of the cramped courtyard, a wedding dances itself out. Windows go successively dark, and only one, on the topmost floor, battles on against the twilight of the September evening. Down below, soles shuffle. A *bubon* bangs, and it sounds as though some lumbering, drunken Samson is stuck in a stone prison—the thwack of heavy footfalls on the yard's stone slabs. In answer to his oafish crashing—the hoarse laugh of an accordion and then, once again, that stubborn, ponderous banging.

Now and again, a flute's voice wafts in—soars up the walls, which resemble the stone shaft of a well. Yet it never reaches the deep-blue rectangle where a lonely star pulses—it breaks off, goes quiet, plunging back into the airless depths of the well just as suddenly as it sprang forth . . .

In the one room where the light is still on, it's nearly twilight. Only there on the desk, as if drawn by a compass—a blinding orb of lamplight: A lamp bows low over a white sheet of paper, as though scanning for something. The thinnest little thread—smoke from a cigarette that's smoldering in an ashtray. No one's there anymore. Save for the dark silhouette of a woman, following a snowy path into the depths of a park, in the room's only picture. And there's also someone in the room's shadows, someone lost in introspection, glancing out of habit at the receding figure—getting smaller, but still not vanishing from the snow-filled expanse . . .

One last time the flute's voice shot upward just as the faraway star was about to touch the upper contours of the stone building. It sailed up the wall, a hair's breadth from that shimmering dot in the sky. Along the same axis, right under the eaves, a window gleamed, slightly ajar. The flute put all its energy, all its desire for open space into that ascent. In its voice trilled the memory of a distant time when Wind—ruler of space, tired of soaring in the sky—would nestle alone in the reeds as the evening's first star appeared in the sky, and the reeds would rustle back, responding to his touch with sweet polyphony. Back in the days of eternal Spring . . .

The thread of smoke that for a moment had seemed immobile in the lamplight illuminating the paper was suddenly tossed about, twirling like a ribbon in the hands of a nimble dancer. And that someone in the shadows approached the window. He noticed that the curtain was trembling, too . . . Suddenly he was struck by the feeling that, besides him and the receding woman, there was a third person in the room, but only for a moment . . . He closed the window and turned off the lamp. The darkness spilling out of the well-like courtyard flooded the room. But outside, things looked brighter: Through the gridded pane that just now had reflected darkness, the wall shone gray . . .

Somewhere in the depths of the universe near the end of the autumnal equinox, one side of the constellation Libra dipped down. But wasn't it dipping all along? Motion, after all, is continuous. Continuing on its course was the same star which, drifting along for centuries, had just peered into the courtyard-well, where the *bubon* banged, the accordion cackled, and, in a sorrowful voice, the restless flute tried to break through to that lofty rectangle of sky. And probably it would have broken through in this final flight if on its way, at the topmost edge of the wall, no window had stood ajar, and no light had shone through it . . .

The Mood

When the theater curtain has not yet risen, when the lights have gone down but not yet out, when the soothing semi-darkness of the hall is supplemented by the similarly muted and *sotto voce* murmur of those who've just entered and those who've already taken their seats, when multicolored spotlights are set up in the side boxes and, as though searching for someone, scan their migratory beams across the curtain and audience, it is then that some of the spectators, without even suspecting it, are taken in by the denizens of the orchestra pit, who by the tuning of their instruments create a singular mood—all in the chaos of remarkably diverse sounds, discordant and indifferent to one another, which will later imitate the most refined harmony of forms within a unified sound structure, though for now each instrument exists in and of itself, representing only the near or distant homeland where it first played, whether testing its abilities in some difficult passage or just proclaiming itself in its unique voice—dozens of voices that simultaneously spill, soar, and slide out of the orchestra pit from beneath fingers, bows, and mallets, racing and chasing one another, bursting out of openings, wooden and brass, large and small: from the dulcet flute with its flowing roulades, to the clarinet, shrill on the highest notes, to the low tuba, plunging to the very bottom; from the tender violin, dainty both in body and voice, to the gargantuan double bass—a chimerical polyphony, which a graceful and shapely harp, belonging to the heavens like the human soul, occasionally breaks, calling for harmony with a silvery arpeggio; and when it seems like the heavy metal gong, erupting and vibrating under the impact of a cloth-muffled wooden mallet, will finally put an end to this raging auditory chaos, in this moment, the maestro gives the signal (his baton against the stand) and the tumultuous whirlwind of voices dissipates like dry leaves swirled by the wind, and, after the prolonged, rustling "shhhh" across the whole keyboard of autumn, the conductor nods as, the oboe, like a high tree, hangs in the silence with its lonely *La*—and right away violins, violas, and cellos respond with their own *La's* surging up and reaching for it, and then, after a roll call of ascending and descending fourths and fifths here come the same roulades, arpeggios, and passages, the same primordial chaos, where all is intermingled—a turbulent, defiant dance of voices—but not for long: As soon as the spotlight snatches the conductor's stand from the semi-darkness, the waiting begins—silence, and after that, with the first wave of the baton, the whole mystery of the mood's creation is dispelled like a waking dream: Some in the audience actually come to the opera anticipating this opening act—which is not usually applauded, except by those not in tune with the mood set by the tuning of instruments before the curtain rises—when an undirected dissemination of voices, each of which seeks only to belong to itself, hurries only to be itself, because soon, obedient to that perfectly tuned *La* (not "me") it will flow into the whole, in service to it alone, singing in its unified voice . . . so each one searches, hurries—before the curtain rises, before the ramp lights come on, and before, backstage, a single resolute and almost ritualistic phrase is uttered, after which the baton's ascent will inevitably follow: "Maestro, on with the show!"

Vigilate!

Once, years ago, I asked to stay the night at a friend's place in order to catch an early train—he lived in Market Square right behind City Hall. From there it was an easy half hour's walk to the railway station (trams didn't run that early), whereas from my place on the outskirts of Lviv, I would have needed to leave the house before sunrise, even though it was summer. I've lived in my share of apartments over the years, but this was my first night in a building like this, on City Hall's doorstep.

It was late when I stepped inside; the sun had already expired above every roof, tower, and steeple, and the pre-autumnal August twilight was seeping through the streets and alleyways below. Beyond the ancient wooden gate through which I entered, it would have been pitch dark, but for a light-bulb dangling all alone from a wire. In its light, intensified by the shadows, the vaulted medieval ceiling carved itself out, and the gray stone slabs led to a wooden staircase, blackened and worn. Climbing from one floor to the next, through the stair-case's bizarre convolutions, so many squashed *o's*, I kept look-ing down, as though into a well growing darker and deeper . . . Overhead, the gabled glass roof was just visible—the same kind that can still be found over some rural wells . . .

As I climbed higher and twilight descended, an indescrib-able feeling congealed in me—a state brought about by what seemed like time's compression, its clotting or sedimenta-tion: Beneath the slabs I'd tread upon entering through the gate were foundations and cellars, more than half a millen-nium old. So, though I was mounting the stairs, I felt like I was plumbing the depths of antiquity, inhaling its aromas—of worn-down stone, of wood, of silence, or rather of the quiet into which the *kamyanytsia* with its hushed inhabitants had plunged. Everything upheld the deepest of all earthly quiet—that of a well . . . Suddenly a jolt of electricity coursed through me. Stepping onto the top floor, I faced the lid of a coffin that lurked like a dark figure—waiting for someone who lay in the apartment next to the one where I was spending the night . . .

We chatted a bit before bed, but not for long since it was late, and I had to get up at dawn. After the customary tea and Lviv pastries, followed by the usual exchange of "Well, good night!" I settled into the sofa that had been made up for me, hoping to get a good night's rest despite the unfamiliar place. But these hopes were in vain . . .

As soon as I got in bed, I began to count the time together with the City Hall clock. To say that I heard its voice every quarter-hour does not begin to describe things: I sensed the clock's peal not so much with my hearing as with my soul, with my entire being, and in its every fiber. I became one giant ear into which the cast-metal words fired like projec-tiles from a catapult: "Vigilate, nescitis enim horam"—Take heed, for ye know not what hour . . . The medieval *kamya-nytsia* seemed to be the ideal echo chamber for that clanging Latin imperative. But, strangely enough, it was not so much the voice that robbed me of sleep, as the person in the neigh-boring apartment who couldn't hear it . . . I tried to imagine how it was possible, in the silence of the night, not to hear the clock's peal. And yet again I understood the futility of such imaginings: Crossing that ultimate border, into the unknown, we bring our sensations with us—but sensations don't exist there.

As I lay listening to my friend's measured breath (he'd fallen right to sleep), I started thinking of various tips for getting to sleep quickly: "Disconnect the brain from external stimuli" . . . But this advice immediately fell away, since I knew no way of "disconnecting my brain." Nor did I know how to "relieve it of all imaginings"—the more I tried, the more clearly I saw the stairwell and the coffin lid, like a dark figure, leaning against the door. One other recommendation was more congenial: "Imagine total darkness. It subsumes everything—a calm, pleasant feeling. Even if some vision tries to surface, the darkness swallows it up, and . . . you fall asleep." I didn't have to imagine darkness, since everything was immersed in it, but those things that surfaced, again and again, preferred not to return to dark obscurity—they kept lingering before my eyes.

Then I turned to my own tried and true methods for inducing sleep. I recalled how, while doing archival work in medeival cells like this one, I spent many months engaged in the highly sophisticated task of "sheet numbering," getting through a few thousand per day. Back then, I'd experienced first-hand the utter futility of opposing sleep's indomitable power. But now, no matter how many sheets I numbered in my imagination, sleep wouldn't come. So, something different: I called to mind a scholar working on documents in the archive's reading room. His research was apparently statistical in nature, and he flipped through piles of documents every day, transcribing numbers from them. He was getting on in years and as he took those numbers down, he whispered: "one thousand four hundred and eighty, one thousand four hundred and eighty-one," etc. And because it was so quiet, that monotone whisper prevailed, pulling everyone else in the room beneath the veil of sleep. In that room, but not this one . . .

Feeling more agitated than relaxed by my efforts at sleep, I began once more to count the hours together with the clock in the tower: It struck one, two, three, four . . . The half and quarter hours sounded in a higher pitch, and the hours in a lower, more reverential tone. Each time it struck—the same admonition: *Vigilate!*—Take heed! As I listened to the alternating silence and ringing, the night trickled by, one minute at a time, seeming to me longer than the longest of winter nights.

In the early dawn before sunrise when, at last, the clock solemnly struck five, I set out for the station to meet my train. Cats roamed the streets between garbage bins—mostly black, as though emanating from the darkness of night. The city was catching a few final moments of sleep. Here and there, street sweepers pottered about with brooms . . . And just an hour later, the sun rose above the city, sweeping from its recesses night's last lingering shadows . . .

Rainy Landscape
with Cat

———————

... The next day, at about the same hour, just shy of noon, he hurried to Cafe Dzyga, "The Spinning Top." Having chosen the same table, on the street, under an expansive umbrella, he ordered a glass of red wine and waited for the cat to appear in the window of a neighboring *kamyanytsia*. The weather was looking up again, at least in his opinion: Though it was early summer, the sky was drawn tight with thunderclouds and sprinkling down a scarcely audible autumnal sort of rain. As he waited, he slipped back, without realizing, to the previous day...

He'd seen her from afar. She was sitting alone amongst the empty tables, though most people would choose to be indoors in such weather. And since he was a little late, she'd already taken a sip of her wine. They ordered another round... She liked this weather, too. She mentioned the cat, which a moment earlier had been sitting in the window, lending an air of coziness to the backdrop of rainy gray. They talked about the rain and about "tomorrow," which only really comes in our imaginations (for as soon as it arrives, it's no longer "tomorrow" but "today"). They talked about this and that—but nothing sad, surely, since she was smiling and laughing. Encouraged by her good mood, he kept chattering on. Later, he reproached himself: In the quiet of a gray, rainy day it's best just to luxuriate in silence.

And then, as though sensing that it was being talked about, the cat reappeared at the window. It was, however, of some breed inimical to good moods. It observed everything not only with a very sour expression, but also a perpetual air of irritated condemnation—"What's the world coming to?" In a word, this was not one of those cats that, surveying the world through a window, "merely responds to movement"—it had its own established worldview. The woman was taken by the narrative of a cat that "merely responds to movement," especially since this cat-observer was meant as a lesson of how not to live: ". . . in the same way, a man"—he was getting to the point now—"may sit for hours at the window, turning his head back and forth—who's going here, who's going there—merely reacting to movement."

But this cat didn't turn its head back and forth—the only movement outside the window was drizzling rain, barely detectable even to a cat's eye. So, after sitting there for a minute, its whole appearance saying "pshaw!" again to the whole visible world, the cat vanished from the window frame—just as quickly as it had appeared, it retired . . . From this moralizing address about how unbefitting it is for humans to act like irrational creatures (like cats), the conversation turned to the difference, more broadly, between animals and humans. The former live, while the latter "re-live"—worrying and endlessly rehashing experiences . . . But this particular cat wasn't so fortunate. It lived a life of leisure, but still couldn't get a life: the world around it was always somehow unsatisfactory and some feeling of disgust or contempt spoiled it all . . .

Listening to the rain's whisper and the touching of glasses, as soft as the tinkling of a tiny bell, admiring the wine's hue, radiant amidst the soft, omnipresent gray, he kept thinking that the whole world was, after all, a spinning top, and that only occasionally, on a drizzling day like today, was it possible to step out of this whirlwind and simply get a life, even for a moment—to react to internal movements that are invisible, elusive, and nearly impossible to record on paper . . . He thought that tomorrow—whether it was real or imaginary—he would come here again, sit at the same umbrella-covered table, so long as it wasn't taken, and "re-live"—he'd live the present day again and again . . . That, after all, was how the first day was lived.

Dead Silence

———

I awoke suddenly in the middle of the night. Something had snatched me from sleep, but at first I couldn't figure out what. Brightness from the moonlit sky poured through the window, and the window grille presented itself as a cross that stretched slantwise over the room, refracting on the wall. The moon itself was no longer visible, but the window's brightly lit top quadrant suggested that just a second ago it had been peering into the room.

This brightness, however, was flowing not so much from the moonlit sky as from the building outside the window; a gray section of its wall, which darkened the room in daytime, had now illuminated it like a huge phosphorizing TV screen that emitted an intense bluish-green light.

In its glow, everything appeared unreal. Objects lost their color and transformed into shadows. Only the window grille stood out, like a strictly proportioned Latin cross drawn in charcoal.

And then I remembered: to begin with, the moon. Before I went to sleep, it had been standing in the window. A perfectly drawn circle, it seemed to linger around the dark crossbeams like a gleaming halo. Behind the moon, a voice. Not words anymore, just the voice alone. The last thing that leaves a person is the psyche, the soul itself, a breath—a measured, muffled sigh.

I observed the moon as it progressed, imperceptibly to the eye. Quietly leaving the center, it hovered above one of the cross's arms, scarcely touching it, then slid along its dark line to the edge of the window. It seemed to me that, on its high trajectory, the moon was accompanied by a low sound—a groan that broke in at perfectly regular intervals. This groan kept getting lower and more muffled, and it also seemed to me that the voice would persist until the end of the cross's arm, where the moon, in all its brilliance, had just arrived.

I was already used to this measured groan because it had gone on uninterrupted for several days and several nights. Wasting away from some incurable disease, my old Polish landlady groaned constantly. The room I rented shared a wall with hers. Since they were connected by a door—boarded up and no longer in use—every single groan, every single word was clearly audible. Words, however, were a rarity: The sick lady's husband, a skinny, hunched little man, was deaf in both ears. In the daytime, they managed to communicate one way or another: The sick lady was still able to get a few words through to the man's consciousness—she pronounced them in his ear. She asked repeatedly whether the water he served her was *gotowana*—boiled for drinking. During the day, there were also visitors—little old ladies. Mostly, they kept quiet, but occasionally you could hear through the door: "Niech pani pomyśli o Jezusie, o Jego Matce . . . Ofiaruj, pani, swe cierpienia Temu, który za nas tyle na krzyżu przecierpiał . . . Tej, która za Nim tyle łez przelała . . . Wtedy te cierpienia staną się dla pani słodyczą . . ."*

---

* Translation from Polish: "And may the lady think of Jesus, of his Mother . . . Offer your sufferings to the One who suffered so much on the cross for us . . . And to the One who shed so many tears for Him . . . Then those torments will become a delight for the lady. . . ."

Things were worse at night. The sick woman made herself known to her husband exclusively by twitching a rope: she held one end, while the other was tied to her husband's arm—he slept across the room from her. But in order to get at least a little sleep, he sometimes freed himself from the rope and tied it to the leg of the bed. Only then did he become submerged—both in sleep and in his deafness.

On that moonlit night, I must have been the only one to notice the sick woman's groaning, measured and constant as though her deliverance lay in this very consistency; and yet, her groaning was becoming more muffled and weaker. I started up to help her, but then remembered that her husband hooked their bedroom door closed at night. Concentrating on that monotonous groan, observing the moon as it slid past the center of the cross, I too finally fell asleep. My brief but deep sleep lasted precisely as long as the moon was traveling from the cross's center to the end of its arm . . .

And so, when I awoke, I stared for some time at the grid of the window, which carved a dark cross in the diffuse, greenish moonlight outside the window—an image of extraterrestrial, cosmic silence. And then I understood: I'd been awakened by the very thing that had lulled me to sleep—the dying woman's groan in tandem with the moon's journey. The groan's presence lulled me to sleep. While its absence woke me up. I knew what this absence meant. I knew but didn't dare to move a muscle. Not only was I afraid, but I reproached myself: It must have been right then, when I'd finally fallen asleep—as the moon was traveling to the end of the cross's arm—that the sick woman grabbed the rope attached to her husband's bed, and in that moment no one was there . . . Absorbed in that unbroken silence, I hesitated. I hoped against hope (and logic) that the sick woman might simply have fallen asleep and that soon she would start groaning again. Allowing for this improbability and being unable to move, I was at the same time sure that I would soon hear my landlord's hurried shuffle down the hallway to my room—and I knew what those steps would mean. And so it came to be . . .

Because I hadn't brought my glasses, the deceased woman's face looked like a pale splotch (the moon was starting to hide itself from view), and in the middle of that splotch was a dark oval—the "o" of her groan. Voiceless now. But still, it needed to be brought to a close by tying the deceased woman's jaw shut. My hands shook—it was my first time so close to death. As I was tying a knot at the top of her head, I saw a few gray hairs caught in it. This disturbed me even more and my insides went completely cold: I was sure I'd hurt her . . .

Now, whenever I hear the phrase "dead silence," I see the dark cross, holding the full moon on its arm; and I hear the measured, muffled groan that is inseparable from that image. I blame myself for that gap in time, along the path that the moon was traveling: from the cross's center to the end of its arm.

The Rainbow over Vyriv

I don't know where the rainbow got the water to make itself beautiful. Probably "borrowed" it from our own Buh River. Its colors, though, those seven shades, definitely came from the sun. Brilliant and washed clean by abundant May rain, it shone before a sprawling dark blue cloud that was retreating eastward, grumbling with thunder and scattering fat silvery drops all around—a sun shower. Against this cloudy backdrop (as the sun stared directly at the rain, blinding it) a seven-colored rainbow—an itty-bitty arch, a cheery archlet, then a colossal curve, a heavenly curvature—rose suddenly above the church, above the village, above the whole land, above the Earth . . .

I have been lucky enough to see a great many rainbows— even double ones—both in the village and in the city, but the one I remember best is this one that I saw in childhood. Even today, I could show you the spot where I stood after running out the door: on the road by the front gate, beside the old, blossoming black locust. I gazed up at the rainbow in amazement, for such miracles don't often occur in the sky (perhaps I was seeing one for the first time), and certainly don't last long. I watched and wondered. All my other senses receded and went quiet so that I did not even smell the black locust's intoxicating aroma—my whole being became sight, wholly immersed in the rainbow's colors that beamed with some kind of otherworldly joy from heaven. I watched, unable to tear my eyes from that harmony of colors, because I knew that such things are fleeting—otherwise they would not be called miracles—and I kept watching . . .

And only now, recalling the image of that distant rainbow, have I understood that, besides sight, another sense must have helped impress that rainbow upon my mind—touch. It wasn't the rainbow I touched, but the Vyriv soil, black and oily from the warm rain. For it is after all from the soil, despite its blackness, that all those celestial colors—of cherries, sunflowers, grasses, cornflowers, and violets—sprouted in the sun's light . . .

The rainbow seems to unite them (and really there is no clear border between colors) as they unfurl on the backdrop of the sky. I not only touched the oily and viscous soil, but kneaded it with my bare foot so that it wormed out, warm, smooth, and vine-like, between my toes.

That rainbow over Vyriv follows me everywhere. I even caught sight of it while translating Ovid: "Iris, the messenger of Juno, clad in robes of many hues, draws up water and feeds it to the clouds."[35] The rainbow draws water, "borrows" it, in order to shine resplendently, so that the people who always say "not now," can look up and catch sight of its splendor through the eyes of their childhood selves, adding to this child's vision all that they have learned since, all the great assets their souls have acquired.

A Jug of Wild Strawberries

An elderly woman brought them to my mother once a year at the height of summer—a jug of freshly picked wild strawberries. She came from a village about seven kilometers away—a village with the ancient name Tadani, so strange it can hardly be connected with anything . . . The woods near there have the same name: Tadani. The jug was filled to the brim with strawberries, covered with fern fronds and tied around the neck with long pieces of grass. As soon as the woman removed the ferns, the room was overtaken by the smell of strawberries.

No words can describe that smell: They only add distance rather than bringing us closer to the incomparable aroma of freshly plucked wild strawberries. In it are the mysteries of nature, the forest, the earth's depths, its life-giving water, without which no plant can rise toward the sun. In the forest, this scent mingles and blurs with many others. Together they create the fragrance of the forest. But nestled together in the closeness of the jug, those wild strawberries smelled only of themselves. They smelled as they once did, in dizzying prehistory, when there was no man to inhale their fragrance, when the ferns were colossal, when dinosaurs trampled the grasses—they were fragrant for their own sake, for their own pleasure . . .

And yet, you could describe that smell as subtle or delicate—like the dainty, low-hanging, and downcast berries themselves, sheltering from the scorching sun beneath a canopy of green leaves. Their aroma, taste, and appearance are the epitome of tenderness and chastity. And speaking of taste, they should only be paired with the barely thickened, not yet sour cream. That's how we used to enjoy those strawberries. The woman would get ready to leave (as my mother showered her with various goods) saying she hoped to bring us another full jug of wild Tadani strawberries next summer. But one summer—I no longer remember when—the woman with the wild strawberries didn't come, and then she never came again . . .

The Garden

Plums wailed and wept blue—
They are cherries no more.
The garden, suddenly elated,
Prays solemnly in silence.

Two, three more apples
plummet, impudent—
The soul hurries home,
or maybe—even further.
(Bohdan Smoliak, *Dictionary of Silence*)[36]

It's true, in the end: wherever the soul finds itself and no matter how good it feels there, a time comes when, before moving onward, it rushes home—to its garden. For what is a home without a garden? The garden is an image of unearthly bliss ("I'll plant a small orchard-paradise," Shevchenko wrote)[37] and, at the same time, of something deeply earthy, rooted in one's own, native soil, where it's cozy and peaceful, where, together with that garden, one can say a prayer, hum a tune, ponder a thought, read, daydream (in a garden, it's pleasant to be alone), and finally even take a nap. For reverie is only a step away from sleep: "Reverie is waking sleep," said the ancients.

The garden is all five of the senses, and it's impossible to favor any one of them. I *listened* to the garden of my youth—to the pelting spring showers beating down on its greenery, to the first fallen leaves rustling underfoot after a scorching August, to the thump of plummeting overripe apples or pears, and further—I listened to the November winds, those "cellos of autumn," whirring in the garden and tearing off the last foliage . . . Just by *touching* their trunks, I could identify those trees even today—whether an apple or pear, sweet or sour cherry, a plum tree or the lone, slender poplar that grew on the garden's edge; it ended up there by some miracle—the single Lombardy poplar in Vyriv.

I *see* every tree from afar and up close—the tireless ants, in a constant rush, scurrying up and down, down and up a trunk, unstoppable in their work; I see a little caterpillar crawling on a cherry branch, but under my touch it immediately transforms into an appendage of that branch—stretches out and freezes at the same angle as the tree's other shoots, identical in color, form, and body. Decades later, translating Ovid's *Metamorphoses* I remembered that strange sight—one body transforming into another in the blink of an eye, just to survive, to endure, to escape the bird's beak . . .

And yet, the garden is its fruit: You "will know the trees by their fruits," we read in the Bible.[38] But the fruit of the earth also embodies all the senses. First, sight: "As the sweet-apple reddens on the bough-top, on the top of the topmost bough; the apple-gatherers have forgotten it—no they have not forgotten it entirely, but they could not reach it"[39] (this is how Sappho saw it—in the lines of one of her wedding songs, she wanted us to marvel at it, at its blushing hue, eternally fresh and captivating. The pear is a giant golden droplet full of thickened malt, frozen above the ground, and about to burst and fall. The perfectly round cherry, which gave its name to that incredible smiling cherry-red shade. The heavy, oblong beads of plums that have soaked up the color of the pre-autumnal sky, already deep blue, and the earth's honey sweetness. For me they conjure up the school mood of late August, when the carefree calm of summer vacations begins to thrum with notes of alarm—"back to school!"—and because of that the garden's sweet comfort seems all the more desirable. High above, the storks are already circling, preparing to depart, bidding farewell to their nests . . .

The garden is generations of men, changing like "generations of leaves":[40] "Graft your pears, Daphnis; your children's children shall gather the fruits you have sown," Virgil wrote, smiling mournfully, in one of his *Eclogues*.[41] So someone (having perhaps read Virgil) planted a pear tree in the middle of the Vyriv parish garden. It had been planted first and was clearly older than the rest. A winter variety: the Bera. In late autumn, my father plucked the pears by tugging on the strings of a special "grabber" tool (a long stick with a metal claw on the end). Then they basked in the hay, yellowing, softening, and filling with malt. We tasted them in winter: an unparalleled flavor, sweet as honey, but not so cloying—this was a subtle sweetness that matched their delicate aroma.

Years later, I recalled those Bera pears while reading Homer, a dialogue between the heroes of the *Iliad*: "But if you're a mortal man, someone who eats earth's fruit, come closer to me, so you can meet your death more quickly."[42] This earth's fruit is, therefore, the destiny of humans, of earthborn

mortals: One must pay for everything, especially sweetness...
There were, besides the Bera tree, two Spasivka pears whose
fruit reached maturity on the Feast of the Transfiguration of
the Lord, a special holiday in Vyriv because our church bore
its name. They were smaller, less prized, and didn't cling so
tightly to the trees: by August, quite a few of them had already
fallen on the ground, and for days bees swarmed around them,
drinking their pulp.

There were also two sprawling cherry trees, as old as the
pears and growing side by side. At harvest time in August,
when the ground cracked from the heat, the red of their
berries deepened a bit (never quite becoming dark-red),
their acidity was perfectly balanced by sweetness, with no
surplus or lack—they weren't short of sweet and thus a tad
too bitter, as the Goliards put it.[43] So we never got sick of
those cherries—they smiled at us, enticed us . . . I'd bring
them to my father with his afternoon snack, when he was
out mowing our wheat plot outside the village, just beyond
Dolynky. There was also a sweet cherry tree that I would sit
in for hours. I loved that spot—it was so high up. The tree's
tiny yellowish berries ripened, blushed, sweetened, with-
out a drop of sourness—that's what makes a sweet cherry,
after all.

Our Vyriv garden is the broad old apple tree that used to
grow at its very edge, near the road, by a small pond—really
just a puddle. Its apples didn't blush red, as in Sappho: The
fruits were green and only in August did they turn slightly yel-
low, signaling that they'd reached maturity and succulence.
I've tried so many apples in my life but never once encountered
such a taste, such a smell. Those apples may not have been red

like Sappho's, but they were just as unattainable, remaining in that garden, of which there is no longer any trace. Nor is there any trace of the deep caterpillar tracks of German tanks. Five of them plowed through our "little paradise" late one night in the summer of '44; perhaps the earth shook and the trees trembled with terror . . . But now there are no more tracks, no garden, no "Tiger" tanks: "Saturn smoothly erases . . ."

The Credenza

It stood in the living room overlooking the garden through one window, and the courtyard through another—by the wall, in a corner where the sun's rays did not reach. It was itself the color of sunshine and that corner always seemed warm and cozy. The lower, more massive part of the credenza had two cabinet doors. Bulkier serving dishes like dinner sets were kept there: large platters, soup tureens and salad bowls, fruit platters, ceramic jugs, compote pitchers, oblong sauce boats (where we're from, "sauce" is pronounced the French way), round cake-stands with feet, and other, mostly porcelain, stuff. Above them, in two drawers, were silver spoons, forks, knives, spatulas for serving slices of cake, and tongs for grabbing them, a corkscrew (father, smiling, would ask in German for the *wie-heißt-er*—the what-chamacallit)[44] and other similar things. On the silverware, in an ornately engraved monogram, one could make out the initials of our great grandmother, Yevheniya Korzhynska.

The upper section of the credenza was smaller. It too had little doors, but with glass panes. The more delicate sets resided there: porcelain and glazed ceramic saucers and demitasses for coffee and tea, wine goblets, a miniature carafe with a set of teensy bulb-shaped liqueur glasses, a small faceted cruet for vinegar, a sugar bowl, a salt bowl with a little silver spoon, and so on. The upper part was only half as wide as the (often marble) surface of the lower one, so there was room for a dish of dry pastries (usually "ammonia cookies") and berries and fruits, when they were in season: grapes, *truskawkas* (strawberries), apples, plums, and other things from the garden. "Go grab it from the credenza" . . . "it's there at the bottom of the credenza" . . . or "it's there on top of the credenza," I hear my mother saying . . .

But for me, above all, the credenza meant coziness, my own little space where no one ever looked. I was privy to that coziness because the credenza did not stand flush against the wall, but rather fenced off a corner of the room, creating a small triangular nook behind it—a little cubbyhole within the room. As a schoolboy, I would squeeze back there, cover the floor with a coarse woolen blanket, nestle in comfortably, and get to reading. This was most pleasurable when it was raining outside the window—or better yet sleeting. But in the corner, it was cozy. That feeling couldn't be created by any old screen, partition, or odd piece of furniture—only by that credenza.

Back then it never occurred to me that the Italian word *credenza* contains the dignified Latin verb *credo*—I believe, I trust, I rely upon. I didn't know that verb, and yet I felt protected, calm, and content behind the credenza's shoulders—I trusted it . . . So sweet was the rain's whisper; and all the sweeter, when it was prolonged and monotone. I hadn't yet realized that I enjoyed solitude. Not oppressive loneliness that shackles a person, but rather the solitude you experience when you know that around you, nearby, there are relatives and friends, that all is well, and you are off by yourself in a tiny nook that no one will peek into: a space that, despite being miniscule, has such expansive horizons. I didn't understand, and couldn't have understood, that real, burdensome loneliness comes when a person is divorced from himself; when a person is on good terms with himself, it's sweet to be on one's own from time to time, so as to be able to bring something back to others ...

I don't remember all the books I read there, but I remember one vividly. It was a historical novel by Mykhailo Starytskyi, *The Robber Karmeliuk*, in four finely illustrated volumes. After finishing the fourth volume, I returned to the first and started over. And this process repeated itself many times ... I feel as though I'm holding one of those volumes now. On the cover, amidst a cloud of dust, the "robber" Karmelyuk gallops on horseback; his companions follow him. I feel the thick (and clothlike) paper of that edition beneath my fingers, turn the pages, and see the sepia illustrations ... I still regret that, just after the war, all four volumes were lost.

Decades later, I picked up the modern single-volume edition of the novel. But I couldn't get back into that old mood with this new edition: There were no illustrations, and there was no nook. I read on, but my soul didn't follow ... Only now, in a library, have I tracked down one volume—the fourth—of that original edition (the others didn't survive). I took it in my hands and felt like I was touching my childhood. For a book is a physical body, not just some letters on a screen. There behind the credenza I loved to read the magazine *Children's World* (a world that was shut down in '39), whose final issues we'd managed to hold onto and which I knew almost by heart. Each time I opened one it felt like the first time because I really was entering a light-flooded children's world.

"How I long for those days of yore ..." sang Lida Korolevych in the post-war years. And for those long-gone days of childhood—our credenza in Vyriv and the nook behind it which, as soon as I opened a book, transformed into a wide, thrilling, and romantic world ...

The String

___

I remember it well: I was still very young, or at least I was still being carried. My head hurt. It hurt so much that I was wailing. Mom and Dad took turns holding me, but nothing helped. Finally, as I lay in Mom's arms, Dad picked up his mandolin and began playing a tremolo. It's not so much the mandolin I remember—its voice or its melody—but the fact that as soon as I heard the plucking of its string, in that very moment, my pain was immediately lifted, as though by an invisible hand. As the saying goes, for every hurt, there's a hand. And the hand that lifted my pain was music . . .

To this day I'm amazed that the sound was not even music, but merely a string responding to a pick—its initial tremolo. How could that momentary touch relieve my headache? Inadvertently, I return to Lucretius, who believed that our sensations[45] of things are individual and can create different impressions, and the first impression always has the greatest power. For the first time, I was hearing the string's voice, for the first time encountering the bottomless enigma of music, which, according to Pythagoras, imitates the harmony of celestial bodies. A tiny crumb, a child in pain, had broken off from that harmony; music brought them back together . . . But, to return to first impressions, the word *impression* comes from the Latin *impressio*, that which leaves an indelible mark, for first is foremost . . .

Human beings get used to things. And that which we're used to no longer impresses. Music, no matter how beautiful, could probably not relieve a headache so instantaneously. Here again, the voice of Lucretius: "For what is ready to hand, unless we have known something more lovely before, gives [incomparable] delight."[46] Speaking about early humans, who were just learning to imitate the cadences of birdsong and listening more broadly to the voices of nature, Lucretius says: "the zephyrs whistling through hollow reeds first taught the countrymen to blow into hollow hemlock-stalks."[47] To me, the string's voice gave incomparable delight (for what could I compare it to?): It was clumsy beneath my father's rough fingers, but so sweet and soothing, that mandolin's tremolo . . .

Corn

My lines and I go round alone.
(Hryhoriy Kochur)[48]

So many times I've picked up a corncob, shiny and smooth with its outer leaves peeled back, and so many times I've admired it. Only now, as I write these words, does it occur to me that corn, by its very appearance, exemplifies order—a golden order. Line upon line, its kernels assume a strict formation, aligned by height from the largest at the base of the cob to the smallest at the top. (For sowing, only cobs of unimpeachable order are selected.) First, however, come the rigid stalks with shiny green leaves, striving toward the sun. Initially, two or three of them shoot up, depending on how many kernels have fallen into each neat furrow. Then, after weeding, only one stalk remains. Together, they're like an orderly green-outfitted army, ready to fight for survival, for growth, for upward progress—toward the sun.

The army is green, yet the alignment is pure gold. It directs all its energy to ensure that the kernels lined up along the cob fill gradually with gold. And whether it's time to harvest that gold—the kernels under the corn's husk—whether the cobs are ready to be broken off, can be seen from the fine blond hair, the tassel, pushing through the leaves at the top of the cob. At first, the hair is pale green, like the kernels beneath the husks (at that stage we cooked the corn and enjoyed it with a little

salt), then blond, and finally golden and dark-brown, no lon-
ger moist, but dry (we used to play with it, making ourselves
mustaches). Finally it's time to break off the heavy corncobs,
filled with nutritious, starchy kernels, two or three cobs per
stalk—the green army has completed its mission: next year,
new kernels will stand up in the same golden formation . . .

At this point, we rip the husks off impatiently like cloth-
ing, from head to toe. The final garment—the very thinnest
leaves—is like an undershirt against the body.

Beneath it, there is gold: smooth, neat, and shiny. The corn
does more than smile—it laughs, flashing all of its pure gold.
The cobs are then tied together by those thinnest leaves—the
little undershirts—and hung from the roof timbers so they'll
dry in the sun, so their gold color will become even purer: the
brightest gold of autumn, its finest smile. Meanwhile, above
the roof, against the sky's deep-blue, the storks trace circles,
bidding farewell to their nests . . . Perhaps I would not be writ-
ing about the corn and would not associate it with order if,
back then, just when the cobs were broken off, my father had
not uttered what might have been the most consequential
words of my life.

One can hardly predict what will save the world—beauty,
shame, or something else—but upon hearing those words,
which scorched me like fire, I was rescued by shame. This is
how it happened. One hot August afternoon, a neighbor boy
and I began playing in the forest of still-intact corn stalks on
our vegetable plot. My father was starting to break off the cobs
and shouted at us to come join in the work (he held physi-
cal labor in the highest regard and considered it man's best
teacher). After showing us how to break off the cobs without

snapping the stalks and where to pile them, he went off on his own, vanishing into the tall, rustling corn—into the husks.

I was sure that my father was gone and began to break the cobs off any which way, even encouraging my friend to be careless: The sooner we finished, I told him, the sooner we could get back to playing. But my father, who was actually standing nearby, overheard me, and, when he returned, hurled the following reproach: "Is that your idea of stewardship?" Not a word more. Many decades have passed since then, but I still hear that question, warning me off the least form of carelessness . . .

On long winter evenings, shucking corn was one of the household chores. That's when those kernels, perfectly aligned and dried by the sun, would rain or rather hail—from one's hand into a basin. And from there—into large woven-straw sacks (that kept the kernels from getting damp). From these, in whatever quantity was needed, they passed beneath the millstone. But first, the kernels were further dried on a griddle pan, on top of the red-hot kitchen stove ("on the *blatte*," as we used to say in our village),[49] so that a stream of hot, loose gold flowed from beneath the millstone—now cornmeal or grits. Only then did the corn give forth its soul, its hidden, tenderly sweet smell: The heat and grinding had released it from its hard casing as if from a golden suit of armor.

And smell is an overture to taste. For isn't what we smell with our nostrils—the most minute corpuscles—the essence of taste? There's a reason why *sapor* means "taste" in Latin, while the same word in the plural *sapores* means "smell": after all, scents disseminate . . . Hot *kulesha*, corn porridge, fragrant steam above a bowl, the smallest, barely detectable "first-beginnings of things" that astonished Lucretius[50] as well as the Ukrainian poet Antonych (who wrote of an "elemental thunderstorm").[51] This fragrant swelter, paired with cold milk, sweet or sour—a spoonful of *kulesha*, followed by a sip of cold sour milk. The fragrant cornmeal loaves baking on the stovetop . . . The smell of childhood, of ancient times and far-away lands . . . And my father's voice . . . I hear it now: "Is that your idea of stewardship?"

Mama's Smile

_____

"Three things," my sister once confessed when we were children, "there are three things that I love most of all: when I wake up and see the coffee grinder on the table, when the sun shines, and when Mama smiles."

How much has been forgotten since then! So many objects, events, so many words, heard and read, have vanished into oblivion—but not my sister's. It's as though she said them yesterday.

I see it now, that wooden coffee grinder standing on the table. Golden-hued, with a shiny nickel top where beans were poured in, it truly warmed our home. In my mind, I give its handle a crank—the shiny little beans crunch as they fall beneath the blade. Fragrant brown powder rains down into the little drawer. As soon as it is pushed out of the grinder, the fine aroma of ground coffee permeates the entire house.

A morning sunbeam reflected on the grinder's nickel top, breaking through the gap in the unlatched window. Everything in the house, all of its myriad objects, were submerged in semi-darkness, in drowsiness, and only the grinder, like an alarm clock, impatiently alerted us that it was daytime outside. Not by its voice, but by its sun-gold hue and the dazzling rays reflected on its top, it announced: "The sun's out!"

So, thanks to my sister's words, I still see that wooden coffee grinder—a kind that's no longer even made. I see a silvery stripe of light extending to the grinder, which smiles in the middle of the table.

Yet my mother's smile somehow slips away from me. I feel as though I'm about to catch it, as though I'm looking right at it . . . But in an instant Mama's smiling face turns sorrowful. That exact sorrowful expression even appeared to me in a dream, long ago, just before my mother had to leave us for eternity: her face heavy with sadness, staring into the distance.

I was younger than my sister and so I saw my mother's smile less often. Maybe that's why I preferred to draw in pencil, while my sister preferred bright, sunny hues. Maybe that's why I love the evening-hour and autumn drizzle, while my sister loves sunrise, clean and smiling through a myriad of dewdrops, as well as spring, with its cheerful major chords.

Still, when I wake up in the morning and recall my sister's words, when I visit our childhood and see that old coffee grinder on the table, then for a while, I keep my eyes closed. I want, as the ancients advised, for my eyes to follow my soul, and not to lead it. I still hope that maybe one day, those transcendent morning rays making their way into the semi-darkness and the wooden grinder gleaming beneath them will guide me back to my mother's smile . . .

The Dance

_____

Hey you, musicians, play me the csárdás,
One last dance before I go.
(From a Lemko song)[52]

That sorrowful story of days past would have been forgotten long ago, it would have passed from memory, were it not for a few vivid details: a white _kozhushok_ coat, a red kerchief, and a woven sash of the same fiery color.

Mountains don't come together but two fields did, once—a larger one extending toward a smaller one. Only a boundary line divided them. To do away with that as well, two people had to come together: the son of the wealthy farmer on the large field and the daughter of the man who farmed the more modest one.

She was forced into the marriage—by her own father and by the man she had to marry to make the field whole. At the church altar, as the priest was joining them as one, she shed a river of tears: Beside her stood a man she didn't love, while the one her heart had chosen—her beloved—was somewhere out in the world, serving in the military.

Shortly after the wedding, he returned from the army. That Sunday, a trio of musicians played at a dance. She took flight from her house like a bird—to see him. They started dancing, as though falling into one another's embrace. So long as the music played, he didn't release her from his arms. And the trio

played like never before, well into the night—just for them:
She thought they'd both die there . . . The *bubon* banged like
an impassioned heart, the violin howled, the cymbals shook
with pity. He told her he was going back to the war. That he
wouldn't return.

After nightfall, her husband drove her home with a beech
switch—for the whole village to see. He beat her day and
night so that she'd love him and forget that other man who'd
returned from the army, then moved on—into the world.
Maybe she would have given in, like so many unlucky girls
had, and submitted to her fate. Maybe . . . Were it not for those
musicians, who'd played for them so fervently throughout that
Sunday dance, of homecoming and of parting, as prolonged
and brief as life itself—*their* dance. She remained the same as
ever—slender and proud. "He can kill me—I'll still never love
him," she'd say.

A white *kozhushok*, a red kerchief, and a woven sash of the
same fiery color. And also a field that, while verdant in spring,
didn't shine with hope, as it once had—but further darkened
her separation.

Notes

1. The two final lines from the Russian writer Ivan Bunin's poem "Pri sveche" (By candlelight).

2. Our rendition of line 465 from Book I of Virgil's *Aeneid* is based on Sodomora's Ukrainian translation. It has been rendered variously in numerous English translations, including those of John Dryden, Frederick Ahl, Stanley Lombardo, H. Rushton Fairclough with G. P. Goold, Robert Fagle, Len Krisak and Christopher McDonough, Shadi Bartsch, and others. Sodomora's understanding of the line most resembles that of Bernard Doering, who translates it thusly: "There are tears at the very heart of things, and the mortal nature of those things troubles the mind of man," Bernard Doering, "Lacrimae Rerum—Tears at the Heart of Things: Jacques Maritain and Georges Rouault," in *Truth Matters: Essays in Honor of Jacques Maritain*, ed. John G. Trapani Jr. (Washington, D.C.: American Maritain Association, 2004), 207.

3. Ray Bradbury, *The Martian Chronicles* (New York: Doubleday & Co., 1950), 53.

4. Virgil, "Eclogue II," in his *Eclogues*, trans. H. Rushton Fairclough, rev. G. P. Goold (Cambridge, MA: Loeb Classical Library, Harvard University Press), 33, line 34, doi: 10.4159/DLCL.virgil-eclogues. 1916.

5. John Amos Comenius, *The Great Didactic of John Amos Comenius*, trans. and ed. Adam M. W. Keatinge (London: Adam and Charles Black, 1907), 43.

6. Seneca, "Epistle XVI: On Philosophy: The Guide of Life," in his *Epistles*, trans. Richard M. Gummere (Cambridge, MA: Loeb Classical Library, Harvard University Press), 107, doi: 10.4159/DLCL.seneca_ younger-epistles.1917.

7. In the original Ukrainian text, the epigraph from Bunin's poem "Evening" was translated by Sodomora himself. Here, we quote the English-language translation by Dmitriy Belyanin: "Translation of Ivan Bunin's Poem 'Evening,'" All Poetry, June 2021, accessed August 21, 2023, https://allpoetry.com/poem/15971699-Translation-of-Ivan-Bunin-s-Poem-Evening-by-Dmitriy-Belyanin.

8. In Book II (lines 58–59) of his *Georgics*, Virgil writes, "O farmers, beyond measure, could they but know their blessings!" Virgil, *Georgics*, trans. H. Rushton Fairclough, rev. G. P. Goold (Cambridge, MA: Loeb Classical Library, Harvard University Press), 169, doi: 10.4159/DLCL.virgil-georgics.1916.

9. A prose translation of Horace's Ode 1.11. Horace, "11. Gather Ye Rosebuds," in his *Odes*, trans. Niall Rudd. (Cambridge, MA: Loeb Classical Library, Harvard University Press), book 1, 45, doi: 10.4159/DLCL.horace-odes.2004. In this story, Sodomora provides his own revised translation of the famous phrase *carpe diem*. In his first 1982 translation of the ode, the forty-five-year-old Sodomora rendered it as "den tsei lovy" (catch this day). But in a much later revised version, he rendered it as "dnia ne zmarnui" (waste not a day), placing more emphasis on ideas of work and legacy. Other English translations of Horace's maxim range from "seize the day" (Jeffrey Kaimowitz, Sidney Alexander, David R. Slavitt), to "seize the moment" (W. E. H. Forsyth) and "harvest the day" (David West).

10. The lines that appear here have been rendered in English via Hennadiy Turkov's Ukrainian translation of Ishikawa Takuboku's Japanese poem. The original poem has been translated into English several times. Shio Sakanishi translates the lines thusly: "I stopped in the midst / Of pulling off my gloves . . . / What was it? / A memory flitted across my mind." Shio Sakanishi, trans., *A Handful of Sand* (Westport: Greenwood Press, 1976), 41. Hiroaki Sato and Burton Watson offer the following version: "Taking off my gloves, my hands stop— / what is it? / a memory flits through my mind." Hiroaki Sato and Burton Watson, trans., eds., *From the Country of Eight Islands: An Anthology of Japanese Poetry* (New York: Columbia University Press, 1986), 452.

11. A reference to Seneca's "Epistle XXII: On the Futility of Half-Way Measures," in his *Epistles*, trans. Richard M. Gummere (Cambridge, MA: Loeb Classical Library, Harvard University Press), 151, doi: 10.4159/DLCL.seneca_younger-epistles.1917. The phrase "fleeting opportunity" also echoes the opening lines of Hippocrates's *Aphorisms*, specifically, the *ars longa, vita brevis* maxim. The opening passage reads, "Life is short, art long, occasion brief, experience / fallacious, and judgement difficult." *The Aphorisms of Hippocrates*, trans. Elias Marks (Glasgow: Collins and Co., 1817), 29.

12. In the sixteenth century, Ivan Fedorov (Fedorovych) was the founder of book printing and publishing in Muscovy and Ukraine.

13. *A Journey to the Sea* (*Die Reise ans Meer*) by Otto Steiger; *The Bread of Those Early Years* (*Das Brot der frühen Jahre*) by Heinrich Böll; *Sunlight on Cold Water* (*Un peu de soleil dans l'eau froide*) by Françoise Sagan; *And Never Said a Word* (*Und sagte kein einziges Wort*) by Heinrich Böll. These titles refer to popular literature published in the 1950–1970s.

14. Arthur Rimbaud's line "Il pleut doucement sur la ville" was the epigraph to the poem "Il pleure dans mon cœur" by his lover, the poet Paul Verlaine. In Anthony Hartley's translation the epigraph reads, "It rains gently on the town." Anthony Hartley, trans., *The Penguin Book of French Verse*, vol. 3: *The Nineteenth Century* (Harmondsworth: Penguin, 1958), 217. In Sodomora's Ukrainian translation the word *doucement* (gently) is interpreted as *quietly*, which is also a possibility in English. It is as if the rain is speaking here (in French *parler doucement* means "to speak quietly").

15. Lviv's Bernardine Monastery, which today is the Ukrainian Catholic St. Andrew's Church. In the Soviet era, the fifteenth-century church was repurposed as the city archive.

16. Ukrainian names consist of first name (e.g., Valentyna), patronymic, an adjectival possessive form derived from the father's name (e.g., Kornylivna), and last name (e.g., Siverska).

17. In the context of this story, *trembita* is simply a part of the choir's name. In other contexts, *trembita* refers to a long horn used as an instrument by Hutsuls (Ukrainian highlanders) in the Carpathian Mountains. A similar instrument is played in Poland, Slovakia, and Romania.

18. Emily Dickinson, *The Complete Poems of Emily Dickinson*, ed. Thomas H. Johnson (Boston: Little, Brown, and Company, 1960), 133.

19. Here and below we offer our bridge translation of García Lorca's poem, based on Mykola Lukash's Ukrainian translation: Federico García Lorca, *Liryka*, trans. Mykola Lukash (Kyiv: Dnipro, 1969), 146.

20. W. S. Merwin's lines reflect an interpretation similar to Sodomora's: "Why was I born among mirrors? / The day walks in circles around me, / and the night copies me / in all its stars." Quoted in Jeffrey McDaniel, "Lorca's 'The Song of the Barren Orange Tree,'" Poetry Foundation, March 15, 2007, accessed August 21, 2023, https://www.poetryfoundation.org/harriet-books/2007/03/lorcas-the-song-of-the-barren-orange-tree.

21. A line from Taras Shevchenko's untitled poem "My vkupochtsi sobi rosly" (We grew up as one). Shevchenko (1814–1861) is the most renowned poet of Ukrainian literature. He is considered Ukraine's

national poet. Saturn is the god of time in Roman mythology. In Greek mythology, he is known as Cronus.

22. Blaise Pascal, *The Thoughts of Blaise Pascal*, trans. C. Kegan Paul from the text of M. Auguste Molinier (London: George Bell and Sons, 1901), accessed August 21, 2023, https://oll.libertyfund.org/title/paul-the-thoughts-of-blaise-pascal.

23. Ibid.

24. A Polish song by Kazimierz Winkler and Philippe-Gérard (Philippe Bloch).

25. Augustine, *The Confessions of Auerilius Augustine*, ed. and trans. Carolyn J.-B. Hammond (Cambridge, MA: Loeb Classical Library, Harvard University Press), 15, doi: 10.4159/DLCL.augustine-confessions_2014.2014.

26. Seneca, "Epistle XXXV: On the Friendship of Kindred Minds," in his *Epistles*, trans. Richard M. Gummere (Cambridge, MA: Loeb Classical Library, Harvard University Press), 245, doi: 10.4159/DLCL.seneca_younger-epistles.1917.

27. Here, Paul Verlaine's line "Le ciel est, par dessus le toit," is rendered via a Ukrainian translation by Hryhoriy Kochur.

28. These two lines come from Sodomora's own poem "Ruka" (A hand). Andriy Sodomora, *Poezia. Proza* (Lviv: Litopys, 2012), 103.

29. Horace, "6. A Crisis in Religion and Domestic Morality," in his *Odes*, trans. Niall Rudd (Cambridge, MA: Loeb Classical Library, Harvard University Press), 163, doi: 10.4159/DLCL.horace-odes.2004.

30. Virgil, *Aeneid*, in his *Eclogues. Georgics. Aeneid: Books 1–6*, trans. H. Rushton Fairclough, rev. G. P. Goold (Cambridge, MA: Loeb Classical Library, Harvard University Press), 355, doi: 10.4159/DLCL.virgil-aeneid.1916.

31. An allusion to Horace, who gave the following advice: "But you will say nothing and do nothing against Minerva's will; such is your judgement, such your good sense. Yet if ever you do write anything, let it enter the ears of some critical Maecius (b) and your father's, and my own; then put your parchment in the closet and keep it back till the ninth year. What you have not published you can destroy; the word once sent forth can never come back (c)." Horace, *Ars Poetica*, trans. H. Rushton Fairclough (Cambridge, MA: Loeb Classical Library, Harvard University Press), 483, doi: 10.4159/DLCL.horace-ars_poetica.1926.

32. From Sodomora's own poem "Zosia and Iwaszko." Sodomora, *Poezia. Proza*, 97.

33. A reference to gladiators who allegedly used this word to greet the emperor before the fight.

34. Propertius, "Elegy 4.7," in Theodore D. Papanghelis, *Propertius: A Hellenistic Poet of Love and Death* (New York: Cambridge University Press, 1987), 149.

35. Ovid, *Metamorphosis*, trans. Frank Justus Miller, rev. G. P. Goold (Cambridge, MA: Loeb Classical Library, Harvard University Press), 21, doi: 10.4159/DLCL.ovid-metamorphoses.1916.

36. Our own translation from Ukrainian.

37. The opening two lines of Taras Shevchenko's poem "L.," in Vera Rich's translation, read: "A house I'll get, a room's due measure / Plant a small orchard-paradise." Taras Shevchenko, *Kobzar*, trans. Vera Rich (Kyiv: Mystetstvo Publishers, 2013), 314.

38. The line from Matthew 7:16 reads "You will know them by their fruits" (NKJV).

39. Sappho, "105a: Syrianus on Hermogenes. On Kinds of Style," in her *Fragments*, trans. David A. Campbell (Cambridge, MA: Loeb Classical Library, Harvard University Press), 131, doi: 10.4159/DLCL.sappho-fragments.1982.

40. Homer, *The Iliad*, trans. A. T. Murray, rev. William F. Wyatt (Cambridge, MA: Loeb Classical Library, Harvard University Press), 285, doi: 10.4159/DLCL.homer-iliad.1924.

41. Virgil, "Eclogue IX," in his *Eclogues*, trans. H. Rushton Fairclough, rev. G. P. Goold (Cambridge, MA: Loeb Classical Library, Harvard University Press), 87, doi: 10.4159/DLCL.virgil-eclogues.1916.

42. Homer, *The Iliad*, trans. Ian Johnston (2010), book 6, line 143, accessed August 21, 2023, http://johnstoniatexts.x10host.com/homer/iliad 6html.html.

43. The goliards were wandering medieval poets known for their satirical verse. Here Sodomora refers to his own translation of a poem by the Archpoet (c. 1130–c. 1165). The adapted line is "quod caret dulcedine, nimis est amarum," which can be roughly translated from Latin as "that which lacks sweetness is too bitter."

44. A reference to Ivan Kotliarevsky's 1819 play, *Natalka Poltavka* (Natalka from Poltava), in which a minor legal official putting on airs repeatedly uses the expression "teye-to yak yoho" ("how shall I put it"). In Sodomora's original, the father asks for the corkscrew using the German filler expression *wie-heißt-er* (a borrowed phrase in western

Ukrainian speech of his generation) and then quotes a similar phrase from Kotliarevsky's play.

45. Lucretius, *On the Nature of Things*, trans. W. H. D. Rouse, rev. Martin F. Smith (Cambridge, MA: Loeb Classical Library, Harvard University Press), 553, doi: 10.4159/DLCL.lucretius-de_rerum_natura.1924.

46. Ibid., 489, line 1413. The word *preeminent* in Rouse's translation has been substituted for *incomparable* to reflect more accurately the coherence of Sodomora's passage, which relies on the idea of comparing. Sodomora uses *compare* in his Ukrainian translation of Lucretius.

47. Ibid., 487, lines 1380–1381.

48. Hryhoriy Kochur was one of the greatest and most prolific Ukrainian translators of the twentieth century. His oeuvre includes translations from twenty-five languages and thirty national literatures. In 1943, he was falsely accused of belonging to the OUN (the Organization of Ukrainian Nationalists) and of distributing nationalist literature by the Stalin regime and sentenced to ten years in a prison camp. The epigraph to this story alludes to the time Kochur spent in the Inta camp in the Komi Republic of Russia.

49. Another example of Sodomora's incorporation of German, most likely a mutated borrowing of the phrase *auf der Platte*.

50. This is a reference to Lucretius's discussion of solid and soft things. Lucretius, *On the Nature of Things*, 47.

51. Bohdan-Ihor Antonych was a Ukrainian imagist poet in the early twentieth century, who described himself as a "pagan in love with life" and a "poet of spring intoxication." The phrase "prapervniv hromovytsia," which we translated as "elemental thunderstorm," comes from his poem "Epichnyi vechir" (Epic evening). In Mark Rudman, Paul Nemser, and Bohdan Boychuk's translation, it is rendered as "the blizzard of splendor." Bohdan Antonych, *Square of Angels: Selected Poems*, trans. Mark Rudman, Paul Nemser, and Bohdan Boychuk (Ann Arbor: Ardis, 1977), 41.

52. Our translation of the two lines from the second stanza of the Lemko song "Ked my pryishla karta" (When I got a draft notice). Lemkos are an ethnic group of far western Ukraine. In this story, Sodomora's characters speak the Lemkos' unique dialect of Ukrainian.

Glossary

Bubon (бубон) [in "The Flute" and "The Dance"]. It is a percussive folk instrument similar to the tambourine.

Historical Archive (Історичний архів) [in "In the Language of Rain" and "The Felled Shadow"]. Its full name is the Central State Historical Archive of Ukraine in Lviv. Opened in 1944, it is the central repository for historical documents dealing with pre-Soviet Western Ukraine.

Kamyanytsia (кам'яниця) [in "The Language of Rain," "The World between the Windowpanes," "*Vigilate!*" and "Rainy Landscape with the Cat"]. It is a type of residential building made of brick or stone, similar to what in Scotland is referred to as tenement. One of the most famous examples is the Chorna Kamyanytsia (Black House) in downtown Lviv.

Kościół (the Polish spelling of *костел*, kostel) [in "*Praesens Historicum*"]. A Roman Catholic Church.

Kozhukh (кожух) or sometimes also **kozhushok** (кожушок), a diminutive form [in "The Dance"]. It is a traditional Ukrainian coat made of sheepskin.

Kulesha (кулеша) [in "People amidst Things" and "Corn"]. Also known as *mămăligă* (Romanian) and similar to Italian *polenta*. It is a dish made of maize flour.

Lemko(s) (лемки) [in "The Dance"]. An ethnic group living in the mountainous region in the most western part of

Ukraine, on both sides of the Carpathians and along the Polish-Slovak border.

Pysanky (писанки) [in "The World between the Windowpanes"]. These are the elaborately painted Easter eggs for which Ukraine is famed.

Spasivka (спасівка) [in "The Garden"]. In this context, it is a type of pear. The word could also stand for a period of fasting in the summer dedicated to the Assumption of the Virgin.

Staroievreiska Street (вулиця Староєврейська) [in "A Room Without Shadows"]. A street in downtown Lviv whose name can be translated as "Old Jewish." It is a testimony to Lviv's multicultural and multiethnic heritage.

Virmenska Street (вулиця Вірменська) [in "The Owl"]. A street in downtown Lviv whose name can be translated as "Armenian." It too is a testimony to Lviv's multicultural and multiethnic heritage.

Vyriv (Вирів) [in "The Owl," "The Rainbow over Vyriv," "The Garden," and "The Credenza]. A small village in the Lviv region, north-east of the city, where Andriy Sodomora was born.

Vysokyi Zamok (Високий Замок) [in "The Felled Shadow," "The Whirligig," and *Praesens Historicum*"]. Often translated as "The High Castle," it is in fact a hill where a castle used to be dating back to the thirteenth and the fourteenth centuries. Today, it is one of the most popular tourist attractions in Lviv, a hill in the park that offers a beautiful panoramic view of the city.

Acknowledgements

The completion of this project wouldn't be possible without the people we've been fortunate to have in our lives. We are grateful to

Roksolana Zorivchak – for introducing us to Andriy Sodomora;

Andriy Sodomora – for giving us permission to translate his wonderful work;

Markiyan Dombrovskyi – for serving as a mediator with the author, answering our questions, and contributing an introduction;

Vasyl Rohan – for providing a wonderful photograph of Lviv for the cover design;

Erín Moure – for editing our work and providing feedback on the most difficult passages;

The Academic Studies Press team, and specifically, Alessandra Anzani, Ekaterina Yanduganova, and Kira Nemirovsky – for working with us on this project;

Peter Jaszi – for edits and his masterly command of English;

The Ukrainian Book Institute – for supporting the project with the "Translate Ukraine" grant;

Vitaly Chernetsky – for editing feedback;

Tabbey Cochrane – for bringing us closer to Sodomora's Ukrainian with her edits;

Mel Bialecki – for proofreading suggestions;

Taras Shmiher – for his expertise on Ukrainian literature;

Mirgul Kali and Ena Selimović of Turkoslavia Collective – for edits, thoughtful discussion, and positivity;

Kate Johnson of Wolf Literary Agency – for sage advice;

Yuliya Zabyelina, Tim Peters, and Svitlana Ivashkiv – for moral support.

About the Translators

Roman Ivashkiv teaches Slavic languages, literatures, and cultures and translation studies at the University of Alabama at Tuscaloosa. His research interests include translation, comparative literature, and language pedagogy. Currently, he is writing a monograph on transmesis (i.e., fictional representation of translation and translators) in contemporary Ukrainian literature and film. With the Canadian writer and translator Erín Moure, he published an English translation of the Ukrainian writer Yuri Izdryk's collection of poetry entitled *Smokes* (2019).

Sabrina Jaszi is a literary translator working from Slavic and Turkic languages. Her recent projects include fantastical writing by Nadezhda Teffi, short fiction by the 1960s Leningrad writer Reed Grachev, and an autobiographical novella by translator-author Semyon Lipkin. She is a co-founder of the Turkoslavia translation collective and an editor of *Turkoslavia* journal, published by the University of Iowa's program in literary translation. In 2022, she received a National Endowment for the Arts Fellowship in literary translation.

Printed in the USA
CPSIA information can be obtained
at www.ICGtesting.com
JSHW020829110624
64551JS00006B/455

9 798887 194387